Thistle & Rose

by Amy Walton

Cover design by Phillip Colhouer & Kayla Ellingsworth
Cover illustration by Michael Ancher
First published in 1895
This unabridged version has updated grammar and spelling.

Contents

Chapter 1
The Picture

A countenance in which did meet
Sweet records, promises as sweet.

WORDSWORTH

A nd so, my dear Anna, you really leave London tomorrow!"
"By the ten o'clock train," added an eager voice, "and I
shan't get to Dornton until nearly five. Father will go
with me to Paddington, and then I shall be alone all the way.
My very first journey by myself—and such a long one!"

"You don't seem to mind the idea," said the governess with a
glance at her pupil's bright, smiling face. "You don't mind leaving
all the people and things you have been used to all your life?"

Anna tried to look grave. "I see so little of Father, you
know," she said, "and I'm sure I shall like the country better
than London. I shall miss *you*, of course, dear Miss Milverton,"
she added quickly, bending forward to kiss her governess.

Miss Milverton gave a little shake of the head as she
returned the kiss; perhaps she did not believe in being very
much missed.

"You are going to new scenes and new people," she said,
"and at your age, Anna, it is easier to forget than to remember.
I should like to think, though, that some of our talks and lessons during the last seven years might stay in your mind."

She spoke wistfully, and her face looked rather sad. As she saw it, Anna felt ungrateful to be so glad to go away and was ready to promise anything. "Oh, of course they will," she exclaimed. "Indeed, I will never forget what you have told me. I couldn't."

"You have lived so very quietly hitherto," continued Miss Milverton, "that it will be a new thing for you to be thrown with other people. They will be nearly all strangers to you at Waverley, I think?"

"There will be Aunt Sarah and Uncle John at the Rectory," said Anna. "Aunt Sarah, of course, I know, but I've never seen Uncle John. He's Father's brother, you know. Then there's Dornton; that's just a little town near. I don't know anyone there, but I suppose Aunt Sarah does. Waverley's quite in the country, with a lovely garden —oh, I do so long to see it!"

"You will make friends, too, of your own age, I daresay," said Miss Milverton.

"Oh, I hope so," said Anna earnestly. "It has been so dull here sometimes! After you go away in the afternoon, there's nothing to do, and when father dines out there's no one to talk to all the evening. You can't think how tired I get of reading."

"Well, it will be more cheerful and amusing for you at Waverley, no doubt," said Miss Milverton, "and I hope you will be very happy there, but what I want to say to you is this: Try, whether you are at Waverley or wherever you are, to value the best things in yourself and others."

Anna's bright eyes were gazing over the blind into the street where a man with a basket of flowers on his head was crying, "All a-blowing and a-growing." In the country, she would be able to pick flowers instead of buying them. She smiled at the thought and said absently, "Yes, Miss Milverton." Miss Milverton's voice, which always had a regretful sound in it, went steadily on, while Anna's bright fancies danced about gaily.

"It is so easy to value the wrong things most. They often look so attractive, and the best things lie so deeply hidden from us. And yet, to find them out and treasure them, and be true to them, makes the difference between a worthy and an unworthy life. If you look for them, my dear Anna, you will find them. My last wish before we part is that you may be quick to see, and ready to do them honor, and to prize them as they should be prized. Bless you, my dear!"

Miss Milverton had felt what she said so deeply that the tears stood in her eyes as she finished her speech and kissed her pupil for the last time.

Anna returned the kiss affectionately, and as she followed her governess out into the hall and opened the door for her, she was quite sorry to think that she had so often been tiresome at her lessons. Perhaps she had helped to make Miss Milverton's face so grave and her voice so sad. Now she should not see her anymore, and there was no chance of doing better.

For a full five minutes after she had waved a last goodbye, Anna remained in a sober mood, looking thoughtfully at all the familiar, dingy objects in the schoolroom. Carpet, curtains, paper, everything in it had become of one brownish-yellow hue, as though the London fog had been shut up in it and never escaped again. Even the large globes, which stood one on each side of the fireplace, had the prevailing tinge over their polished, cracked surfaces. As Anna's eye fell on these, her heart gave a sudden bound of joy. She would never have to do problems again! She would never have to pass any more dull hours in this room, with Miss Milverton's grave face opposite to her, and the merest glimpses of sunshine peering in now and then over the brown blinds. No more sober walks in Kensington Gardens, where she had so often envied the ragged children, who could play about, and laugh, and run, and do as they liked. There would be freedom now, with green fields, flowers, and companions perhaps of her own age. Everything new, everything gay and bright, no more dullness, no more tedious days—after all, she was glad, very glad!

It was so pleasant to think of that she could not help dancing round and round the big table all alone, snapping her fingers at the globes as she passed them. When she was tired, she flung herself into Miss Milverton's brown leather chair and looked up at the clock, which had gone soberly on its way as though nothing were to be changed in Anna's life. She felt provoked with its placid face. "Tomorrow at this time," she said to it, half aloud, "I shan't be here, and Miss Milverton won't be here, and I shall be seeing new places and new people, and— oh, I do wonder what it will be like!"

The clock ticked steadily on, regardless of anything but its own business. Half-past six! Miss Milverton had stayed longer than usual. Anna began to wonder what time her father would be home. They were to dine together on this, their last evening, but Mr. Forrest was so absorbed in his preparations for leaving England that he was likely to be very late. Perhaps he would not be in till eight o'clock, and even then he would have his mind too full of business to talk much at dinner and would spend the evening in writing letters. Anna sighed. There were some questions she very much wanted to ask him, and this would be her only chance. Tomorrow she was to go to Waverley, and the next day Mr. Forrest started for America, and she would not see him again for two whole years.

It was strange to think of, but not altogether sad from Anna's point of view, for her father was almost a stranger to her. He lived a life apart, into which she had never entered. His friends, his business, and his frequent journeys abroad occupied him fully, and he was quite content that Anna's welfare should be left in the hands of Miss Milverton, her daily governess. It was Aunt Sarah who recommended Miss Milverton to the post, which she had now filled, with ceaseless kindness and devotion, for seven years. "You will find her invaluable," Mrs. Forrest had said to her brother-in-law, and so she was. When Anna was ill, she nursed her. When she wanted a change of air, she took her to the seaside. She looked after her, both in body and mind, with the utmost conscientiousness. But there was one thing she could not do: she could not be an amusing companion for a girl of fifteen, and Anna had often been lonely and dull.

Now that was all over. A sudden change had come into her life. The London house was to be given up, her father was going away, and she was to be committed to Aunt Sarah's instruction and care for two whole years. Waverley and Aunt Sarah, instead of London and Miss Milverton! It was a change indeed, in more than one way; for although Anna was nearly fifteen, she had never yet stayed in the country. Her ideas of it were gathered from books and what she could see from a railway carriage, as Miss Milverton and she were carried swiftly on their way to the seaside for their annual change of air. She thought of it all now as she sat musing in the old brown chair.

It had often seemed strange that Aunt Sarah, who arranged everything and to whom appeal was always made in matters which concerned Anna, should never have asked her to stay at Waverley before. Certainly there were no children at the rectory, but still, it would have been natural, she thought, for was not Uncle John her father's own brother, and she had never even seen him!

Aunt Sarah came to London occasionally and stayed the night, and had long talks with Mr. Forrest and Miss Milverton, but she had never hinted at a visit from Anna.

When, a little later, her father came bustling in, with a pre-occupied pucker on his brow and his most absent manner, she almost gave up the idea of asking questions. Dinner passed in perfect silence, and she was startled when Mr. Forrest suddenly mentioned the very place that was on her mind.

"Well, Anna," he said, "I've been to Waverley today."

"Oh, Father, have you?" she answered eagerly.

Mr. Forrest sipped his wine reflectively.

"How old are you?" he asked.

"Fifteen next August," replied Anna.

"Then," he continued, half to himself, "it must be over sixteen years since I saw Waverley and Dornton."

"Are they just the same?" asked his daughter. "Are they pretty places?"

"Waverley's pretty enough. Your Uncle John has built another room, and spoiled the look of the old house, but that's the only change I can see."

"And Dornton," said Anna, "what is that like?"

"Dornton," said Mr. Forrest absently, "Dornton is the same dull little hole of a town I remember."

"Oh," said Anna in a disappointed voice.

"There's a fine old church, though, and the river's nice enough. I used to know every turn in that river. Well," rising abruptly and leaning his arm against the mantelpiece, "it's a long while ago—a long while ago—it's like another life."

"Did you stay often at Waverley?" Anna ventured to ask presently.

Mr. Forrest had fallen into a daydream, with his eyes fixed on the ground. He looked up when Anna spoke as though he had forgotten her presence.

"It was there I first met your mother," he said, "or rather, at Dornton. We were married in Dornton church."

"Oh," said Anna, very much interested, "did mother live at Dornton? I never knew that."

"And that reminds me," said Mr. Forrest, taking a leather case out of his pocket, and speaking with an effort, "I've something I want to give you before you go away. You may as well have it now. Tomorrow we shall be both in a hurry. Come here."

He opened the case and showed her a small, round portrait painted on ivory. It was the head of a girl of eighteen, exquisitely fair, with sweet, modest-looking eyes. "Your mother," he said briefly.

Anna almost held her breath. She had never seen a picture of her mother before and had very seldom heard her mentioned.

"How lovely!" she exclaimed. "May I really have it to keep?"

"I had it copied for you from the original," said Mr. Forrest.

"Oh, Father, thank you so much," said Anna earnestly. "I do so love to have it."

Mr. Forrest turned away suddenly and walked to the window. He was silent for some minutes, and Anna stood with the case in her hand not daring to speak to him. She had an instinct that it was a painful subject.

"Well," he said at last, "I need not tell you to take care of it. When I come back you'll be nearly as old as she was when that was painted. I can't hope more than that you may be half as good and beautiful."

Anna gazed earnestly at the portrait. There were some words in tiny letters beneath it: "Priscilla Goodwin," she read, "aged eighteen."

Priscilla! A soft, gentle sort of name, which seemed to suit the face.

If Father wanted me to look like this, she thought to herself, he shouldn't have called me Anna. How could anyone named Anna grow up so pretty!

"Why was I named Anna?" she asked.

"It was your mother's wish," replied Mr. Forrest. "I believe it was her mother's name."

"Is my grandmother alive?" said Anna.

"No, she died years before I ever saw your mother. Your grandfather, old Mr. Goodwin, is living still—at Dornton."

"At Dornton!" exclaimed Anna in extreme surprise. "Then why don't I go to stay with him while you're away, instead of at Waverley?"

"Because," said Mr. Forrest, turning from the window to face his daughter, "it has been otherwise arranged."

Anna knew that tone of her father's well; it meant that she had asked an undesirable question. She was silent, but her eager face showed that she longed to hear more.

"Your grandfather and I have not been very good friends," said Mr. Forrest at length, "and have not met for a good many years—but you're too young to understand all that. He lives in a very quiet sort of way. Once, if he had chosen, he might have risen to a different position. But he didn't choose, and he remains what he has been for the last twenty years—organist of Dornton church. He has great musical talent, I've always been told, but I'm no judge of that."

These new things were quite confusing to Anna; it was difficult to realize them all at once. The beautiful, fair-haired mother, whose picture she held in her hand, was not so strange. But her grandfather! She had never even heard of his existence, and now she would very soon see him and talk to him. Her thoughts, hitherto occupied with Waverley and the rectory, began to busy themselves with the town of Dornton, the church where her mother had been married, and the house where she had lived.

"Aunt Sarah knows my grandfather, of course," she said aloud. "He will come to Waverley, and I shall go sometimes to see him at Dornton?"

"Oh, no doubt, no doubt, your aunt will arrange all that," said Mr. Forrest wearily. "And now you must leave me, Anna. I've no time to answer any more questions. Tell Mary to take a lamp into the study and bring me coffee. I have heaps of letters to write and people to see this evening."

"Your aunt will arrange all that!" What a familiar sentence that was. Anna had heard it so often that she had come to look upon Aunt Sarah as a person whose whole office in life was to arrange and settle the affairs of other people, and who was sure to do it in the best possible way.

When she opened her eyes the next morning, her first movement was to feel under her pillow for the case which held the picture of her mother. She had a half fear that she might have dreamt all that her father had told her. No. It was real. The picture was there. The gentle face seemed to smile at her as she opened the case. How nice to have such a beautiful mother! As she dressed, she made up her mind that she would go to see her grandfather directly when she got to Waverley. What would he be like? Her father had spoken of his musical talent in a half-pitying sort of way. Anna was not fond of music, and she very much hoped that her grandfather would not be too much wrapped up in it to answer all her questions. Well, she would soon find out everything about him. Her reflections were hurried away by the bustle of departure, for Mr. Forrest, though he traveled so much, could never start on a journey without agitation and fuss, and fears as to losing his train. So, for the next hour, until Anna was safely settled in a through carriage for Dornton, with her ticket in her purse, a benevolent old lady opposite to her, and the guard prepared to give her every attention, there was no time to realize anything, except that she must make haste.

"Well, I think you're all right now," said Mr. Forrest, with a sigh of relief, as he rested from his exertions. "Look out for your aunt on the platform at Dornton. She said she would meet you herself. Why," looking at his watch, "you don't start for six minutes. We needn't have hurried after all. Well, there's no object in waiting, as I'm so busy, so I'll say goodbye now. Remember to write when you get down. Take care of yourself."

He kissed his daughter and was soon out of sight in the crowded station. Anna had now really begun her first journey out into the world.

Chapter 2

Dornton

A bird of the air shall carry the matter.
ECCLESIASTES 10:20

On the same afternoon as that on which Anna was traveling towards Waverley, Mrs. Hunt, the doctor's wife in Dornton, held one of her working parties. This was not at all an unusual event, for the ladies of Dornton and the neighborhood had undertaken to embroider some curtains for their beautiful old church, and this necessitated a weekly meeting of two hours, followed by the refreshment of tea and conversation. The people of Dornton were fond of meeting in each other's houses and very sociably inclined. They met to work, they met to read Shakespeare, they met to sing and to play the piano, they met to discuss interesting questions, and they met to talk. It was not, perhaps, so much what they met to do that was the important thing, as the fact of meeting.

"So pleasant to *meet*, isn't it?" one lady would say to the other. "I'm not very musical, you know, but I've joined the glee society because it's an excuse for *meeting*."

And, certainly, of all the houses in Dornton where these meetings were held, Dr. Hunt's was the favorite. Mrs. Hunt was so amiable and pleasant, the tea was so excellent, and the conversation of a most superior flavor. There was always the chance, too, that the doctor might look in for a moment at teatime, and though he was discretion itself and never gossiped about his patients, it was interesting to gather from his face whether he was anxious, or the reverse, as to any special case.

This afternoon, therefore, Mrs. Hunt's drawing room presented a busy and animated scene. It was a long, low room, with French windows, through which a pleasant old garden, with a wide lawn and shady trees, glimpses of red roofs beyond, and a church tower, could be seen. Little tables were placed at convenient intervals, holding silk, scissors, cushions full of needles and pins, and all that could be wanted for the work in hand, which was to be embroidered in separate strips. Over these many ladies were already deeply engaged, though it was quite early and there were still some empty seats.

"Shall we see Mrs. Forrest this afternoon?" asked one of those who sat near the hostess at the end of the room.

"I think not," replied Mrs. Hunt, as she greeted a newcomer. "She told me that she had to drive out to Losenick about the character of a maid-servant."

"Oh, well," returned the other with a little shake of the head, "even Mrs. Forrest can't manage to be in two places at once, can she?"

Mrs. Hunt smiled and looked pleasantly around at her assembled guests but did not make any other answer.

"Although, I was only saying this morning, there's very little Mrs. Forrest can't do if she makes up her mind to it," resumed Miss Gibbins, the lady who had first spoken. "Look at all her arrangements at Waverley! It's well known that she manages the schools almost entirely. And then her house—so elegant, so orderly—and such a way with her maids! *Some* people consider her a little stiff in her manner, but I don't *know* that I should call her that."

She glanced inquiringly at Mrs. Hunt, who still smiled and said nothing.

"It's not such a very difficult thing," said Mrs. Hurst, the wife of the curate of Dornton, "to be a good manager, or to have good servants, if you have plenty of money." She pressed her lips together rather bitterly, as she bent over her work.

"There was one thing, though," pursued Miss Gibbins, dropping her voice a little, "that Mrs. Forrest was not able to prevent, and that was her brother-in-law's marriage. I happen to know that she felt that very much. And it *was* a sad mistake altogether, wasn't it?"

She addressed herself politely to Mrs. Hunt, who was gazing serenely out into the garden, and that lady murmured in a soft tone.

"Poor Prissy Goodwin! How pretty and nice she was!"

"Oh, as to that, dear Mrs. Hunt," broke in a stout lady with round eyes and a very deep voice, who had newly arrived, "that's not quite the question. Poor Prissy was very pretty, and very nice and refined, and as good as gold. We all know that. But *was* it the right marriage for Mr. Bernard Forrest? An organist's daughter, or you might even say, a music master's daughter!"

"Old Mr. Goodwin has aged very much lately," remarked Mrs. Hunt. "I met him this morning, and he looked so tired that I made him come in and rest a little. He had been giving a lesson to Mrs. Palmer's children out at Pynes."

"How kind and thoughtful of you, dear Mrs. Hunt," said Miss Gibbins. "That's very far for him to walk. I wonder he doesn't give it up. I suppose, though, he can't afford to do that."

"I don't think he has ever been the same man since Prissy's marriage," said Mrs. Hunt, "though he plays the organ more beautifully than ever."

With her spectacles perched upon her nose, her hands crossed comfortably on her lap, and a most beaming smile on her face, Mrs. Hunt looked the picture of contented idleness, while her guests stitched away busily with flying fingers and heads bent over their work. She had done about half an inch of the pattern on her strip, and now, her needle being unthreaded, made no attempt to continue it.

"Delia's coming in presently," she remarked placidly, meeting Miss Gibbins' sharp glance as it rested on her idle hands. "She will take my work a little while—ah, here she is," as the door opened.

A girl of about sixteen came towards them, stopping to speak to the ladies as she passed them on her way up the room. She was short for her age and rather squarely built, holding herself very upright and walking with calmness and decision.

Everything about Delia Hunt seemed to express determination, from her firm chin to her dark curly hair, which would always look rough, although it was brushed back from her forehead and fastened up securely in a knot at the back of her head. Nothing could make it lie flat and smooth, however, and in spite of all Delia's efforts, it curled and twisted itself defiantly wherever it had a chance. Perhaps, by doing so, it helped to soften a face which would have been a little hard without the good tempered expression which generally filled the bright brown eyes.

"That sort of marriage never answers," said Mrs. Winn as Delia reached her mother's side. "Just see what unhappiness it caused. It was a bitter blow to Mr. and Mrs. Forrest; it made poor old Mr. Goodwin miserable and separated him from his only child; and as to Prissy herself—well, the poor thing didn't live to find out her mistake and left her little daughter to feel the consequences of it."

"Poor little motherless darling," murmured Mrs. Hunt. "Del, my love, go on with my work a little, while I say a few words to old Mrs. Crow."

Delia took her mother's place, threaded her needle, raised her eyebrows with an amused air as she examined the work accomplished, and bent her head industriously over it.

"Doesn't it seem quite impossible," said Miss Gibbins, "to realize that Prissy's daughter is really coming to Waverley tomorrow! Why, it seems the other day that I saw Prissy married in Dornton church!"

"It must be fifteen years ago at the least," said Miss Winn in such deep tones that they seemed to roll around the room. "The child must be fourteen years old."

"She wore gray cashmere," said Miss Gibbins reflectively, "and a little white bonnet. And the sun streamed in upon her through the painted window. I remember thinking she looked like a dove. I wonder if the child is like her."

"The Forrests have never taken much notice of Mr. Goodwin, since the marriage," said Mrs. Hurst, "but I suppose, now his grandchild is to live there, all that will be altered."

Delia looked quickly up at the speaker, but she checked the words on her lips and said nothing.

"You can't do away with the ties of blood," said Mrs. Winn. "The child's his grandchild. You can't ignore that."

"Why should you want to ignore it?" asked Delia, suddenly raising her eyes and looking straight at her.

The attack was so unexpected that Mrs. Winn had no answer ready. She remained speechless, with her large, gray eyes wider open than usual for quite a minute before she said, "These are matters, Delia, which you are too young to understand."

"Perhaps I am," answered Delia, "but I can understand one thing very well, and that is that Mr. Goodwin is a grandfather that anyone ought to be proud of, and that if his relations are not proud of him, it is because they are not worthy of him."

"Oh, well," said Miss Gibbins, shaking her head rather nervously as she looked at Delia, "we all know what a champion Mr. Goodwin has in you, Delia. 'Music with its silver sound' draws you together, as Shakespeare says. And, of course, we're all proud of our organist in Dornton, and, of course, he has great talent. Still, you know, when all's said and done, he *is* a music master, and in quite a different position from the Forrests."

"Socially," said Mrs. Winn, placing her large, white hand flat on the table beside her to emphasize her words, "Mr. Goodwin is not on the same footing. When Delia is older, she will know what that means."

"I know it now," replied Delia. "I never consider them on the same footing at all. There are plenty of clergymen everywhere, but where could you find anyone who can play the violin like Mr. Goodwin?"

She fixed her eyes with innocent inquiry on Mrs. Winn. Mrs. Hurst bridled a little.

"I do think," she said, "that clergymen occupy a position quite apart. I like Mr. Goodwin very much. I've always thought him a nice old gentleman, and Herbert admires his playing, but—"

"Of course, of course," said Mrs. Winn, "we must be all agreed as to that. You're too fond, my dear Delia, of giving your opinion on subjects where ignorance should keep you silent. A girl of your age should try to behave herself, lowly and reverently, to all her betters."

"So I do," said Delia, with a smile. "In fact, I feel so lowly and reverent sometimes that I could almost worship Mr. Goodwin. I am ready to humble myself to the dust when I hear him playing the violin."

Mrs. Winn was preparing to make a severe answer to this, when Miss Gibbins, who was tired of being silent, broke adroitly in and changed the subject.

"You missed a treat last Thursday, Mrs. Winn, by losing the Shakespeare reading. It was rather far to get out to Pynes, to be sure, but it was worth the trouble to hear Mrs. Hurst read *Arthur.*"

The curate's wife gave a little smile, which quickly faded as Miss Gibbins continued, "I had no idea there was anything so touching in Shakespeare. Positively melting! And then Mrs. Palmer looked so well! She wore that rich plum-colored silk, you know, with handsome lace, and a row of most beautiful lockets. I thought to myself, as she stood up to read in that sumptuous drawing room, that the effect was regal. 'Regal,' I said afterward, 'is the only word to express Mrs. Palmer's appearance this afternoon.'"

"What part did Mrs. Palmer read?" asked Delia, as Miss Gibbins looked around for sympathy.

"Let me see. Dear me, it's quite escaped my memory. Ah, I have it. It was the mother of the poor little boy, but I forget her name. You will know, Mrs. Hurst; you have such a memory!"

"It was Constance," said the curate's wife. "Mrs. Palmer didn't do justice to the part. It was rather too much for her. Indeed, I don't consider that they arranged the parts well last time. They gave my husband nothing but 'messengers,' and the vicar had 'King John.' Now, I don't want to be partial, but I think most people would agree that Herbert reads Shakespeare *rather* better than the vicar."

"I wonder," said Miss Gibbins, turning to Delia as the murmur of assent to this speech died away, "that you haven't joined us yet, but I suppose your studies occupy you at present."

"But I couldn't read aloud, in any case, before a lot of people," said Delia, "and Shakespeare must be so very difficult."

"You'd get used to it," said Miss Gibbins. "I remember," she said with a little laugh, "how nervous *I* felt the first time I stood up to read. My heart beat so fast I thought it would choke me. The first sentence I had to say was, 'Cut him in pieces!' and the words came out quite in a whisper. But now I can read long speeches without losing my breath or feeling at all uncomfortable."

"I like the readings," said Mrs. Hurst, "because they keep up one's knowledge of Shakespeare, and that *must* be refining and elevating, as Herbert says."

"So pleasant, too, that the clergy can join," added Miss Gibbins.

"Mrs. Crow objects to that," said Mrs. Hurst. "She told me once she considered it wrong because they might be called straight away from reading plays to attend a deathbed. Herbert, of course, doesn't agree with her, or he wouldn't have helped to get them up. He has a great opinion of Shakespeare as an elevating influence, and though he *did* write plays, they're hardly ever acted. He doesn't seem, somehow, to have much to do with the theater."

"Between ourselves," said Miss Gibbins, sinking her voice and glancing to the other end of the room, where Mrs. Crow's black bonnet was nodding confidentially at Mrs. Hunt, "dear old Mrs. Crow is *rather* narrow-minded. I should think the presence of the vicar at the readings might satisfy her that all was right."

"The presence of *any* clergyman," began Mrs. Hurst, "ought to be sufficient warrant that—"

But her sentence was not finished, for at this moment a general rustle at the further end of the room, the sudden ceasing of conversation, and the door set wide open showed that it was time to adjourn for tea. Work was rolled up, thimbles and scissors put away in work bags, and very soon the whole assembly had floated across the hall into the dining room and was pleasantly engaged upon Mrs. Hunt's hospitable preparations for refreshment. Brisk little remarks filled the air as they stood about with their teacups in their hands.

"I never can resist your delicious scones, Mrs. Hunt. Homemade? You don't say so. I wish my cook could make them—"

"Thank you, Delia, I *will* take another cup of coffee. Yours is always so good—"

"Such a pleasant afternoon! Dear me, nearly five o'clock? How time flies—"

"Dr. Hunt very busy? Fever in Back Row? So sorry. But decreasing? So glad—"

"Goodbye, *dear* Mrs. Hunt. We meet next Thursday, I hope?—"

And so on, until the last lady had said farewell and smiled affectionately at her hostess, and a sudden silence fell on the room left in the possession of Delia and her mother.

"Del, my love," said the latter caressingly, "go and put the drawing room straight, and see that all those things are cleared away. I will try to get a little nap. Dear old Mrs. Crow had so much to tell me that my head quite aches."

Delia went into the deserted drawing room where the chairs and tables, standing about in the little groups left by their late occupiers, still seemed to have a confidential air, as though they were telling each other interesting bits of news. She moved about with a preoccupied frown on her brow, picking up morsels of silk from the floor, rolling up strips of serge, and pushing back chairs and tables, until the room had regained its ordinary look. Then she stretched her arms above her head, gave a sigh of relief, and strolled out of the open French windows into the garden. The air was very calm and still so that various mingled noises from the town could be plainly heard, though not loudly enough to produce more than a subdued hum, which was rather soothing than otherwise. Amongst them, the deep recurring tones of the church bell, ringing for evening prayers, fell upon Delia's ear as she wandered slowly up the gravel path, her head full of busy thoughts.

They were not wholly pleasant thoughts, and they had to do chiefly with two people, one very well known to her, and the other quite a stranger—Mr. Goodwin and his grandchild, Anna Forrest. Delia could hardly make up her mind whether she were pleased or annoyed at the idea of Anna's arrival. Of course, she was glad, she told herself, of anything that would please the "Professor," as she always called Mr. Goodwin, and she was curious and anxious to see what the newcomer would be like, for perhaps they might be companions and friends, though Anna was two years younger than herself. She could not, however, prevent a sort of suspicion that made her feel uneasy. Anna might be proud. She might even speak of the Professor in the condescending tone which so many people used in Dornton. Mrs. Forrest at Waverley always looked proud, Delia thought. Perhaps Anna would be like her.

"If she is," said Delia to herself, suddenly stopping to snap off the head of a snapdragon which grew in an angle of the old red wall, "if she is, if she dares, if she doesn't see that the Professor is worth more than all the people in Dornton, I *will* despise her. I will—"

She stopped and shook her head.

"And if it's the other way, and she loves and honors him as she ought, and is everything to him, and, and, takes my place, what shall I do then? Why, then, I will try not to detest her."

She laughed a little as she stooped to gather some white pinks which bordered the path and fastened them in her dress.

"Pretty she is sure to be," she continued to herself, "like her mother, whom they never mention without praise—and she is almost certain to love music. Dear old Professor, how pleased he will be! I will try not to mind, but I do hope she can't play the violin as well as I do. After all, it would be rather unfair if she had a beautiful face and a musical soul as well."

The bell stopped, and the succeeding silence was harshly broken by the shrill whistle of a train.

"There's the five o'clock train," said Delia to herself. "Tomorrow by this time she will be here."

Mrs. Winn and Miss Gibbins, meanwhile, had pursued their way home together, for they lived close to each other.

"It's a pity Delia Hunt has such blunt manners, isn't it?" said the latter regretfully, "and such very decided opinions for a young girl? It's not at all becoming. I felt quite uncomfortable just now."

"She'll know better by-and-by," said Mrs. Winn. "There's a great deal of good in Delia, but she is conceited and self-willed, like all young people."

Miss Gibbins sighed. "She'll never be so amiable as her dear mother," she said. "Why!" suddenly changing her tone to one of surprise, "isn't that Mr. Oswald?"

"Yes, I think so," said Mrs. Winn, gazing after the spring-cart which had passed them rapidly. "What then?"

"He had a *child* with him," said Miss Gibbins impressively.

"A child with fair hair, like Prissy Goodwin's, and they came from the station. Something tells me it was Prissy's daughter."

"Nonsense, Julia," replied Mrs. Winn. "She's not expected till tomorrow. Mrs. Forrest told Mrs. Hunt so herself. Besides, how should Mr. Oswald have anything to do with meeting her? That was his own little girl with him, I daresay."

"Daisy Oswald has close-cropped, black hair," replied Miss Gibbins, quite unshaken in her opinion. "This child was older, and her hair shone like gold. I feel sure it was Prissy's daughter."

Chapter 3

Waverley

Meadows trim with daisies pied,
Shallow brooks and rivers wide.

MILTON

While this went on at Dornton, Anna was getting nearer and nearer to her new home. At first, she was pleased and excited at setting forth on a journey all by herself, and found plenty to occupy her with all she saw from the carriage windows, and with wondering which of the villages and towns she passed so rapidly were like Dornton and Waverley. It was surprising that the old lady opposite her could look so placid and calm. Perhaps, however, she was not going to a strange place amongst new people, and most likely she had taken a great many journeys already in her life. Anna was glad this was not her own case. It must be very dull, she thought, to be old and to have gotten used to everything, and to have almost nothing to look forward to.

As the day wore on, and the hot afternoon sun streamed in at the windows, the old lady, who was her only companion, fell fast asleep, and Anna began to grow rather weary. She took the case with her mother's picture on it out of her pocket and studied it again attentively. The gentle, sweet face seemed to smile back kindly at her. "If you are half as beautiful and a quarter as good," her father had said. Was she at all like the picture now? Anna wondered. Surely her hair was rather the same color. She pulled a piece of it around to the front—it was certainly yellow but hardly so bright. Well, her grandfather would tell her. She would ask him on the very first opportunity. Her grandfather! It was wonderful to think she should really see him soon and ask him all sorts of questions about her mother. He lived at Dornton, but that was only two miles from Waverley, and, no doubt, she should often be able to go there. He was an organist.

Her father's tone, half-pitying, half-disapproving, came back to her with the word. She tried to think of what she knew about organists. It was not much. There was an organist in the church in London to which she had gone every Sunday with Miss Milverton, but he was always concealed behind red curtains so that she did not even know what he looked like. The organist must certainly be an important person in a church. Anna did not see how the service could get on without him. What a pity that her grandfather did not play the organ in her uncle John's church, instead of at Dornton!

She made a great many resolves as she sat there with her mother's portrait in her hand. She would be very fond of her grandfather, and, of course, he would be very fond of her; and as he lived all alone, there would be a great many things she could do to make him happier. She pictured herself becoming very soon his chief comforter and companion, and she began to wonder how he had done without her so long.

Lost in these thoughts, she hardly noticed that the train had begun to slacken its pace. Presently, it stopped at a large station. The old lady roused herself, tied her bonnet strings, and evidently prepared for a move.

"You're going farther, my dear," she said kindly. "Dornton is the next station. You won't mind being alone a little while?"

She nodded and smiled from the platform. Anna handed out her numerous parcels and baskets. The train moved on, and she was now quite alone. She might really begin to look out for Dornton, which must be quite near. It seemed a long time coming, however, and she had made a good many false starts, grasping her rugs and umbrella, before there was an unmistakable shout of "Dornton!" She got out and looked up and down the platform, but it was easy to see that Mrs. Forrest was not there. Two porters, a newspaper boy, and one or two farmers were moving about in the small station, but there was no one in the least like Aunt Sarah. Anna stood irresolute. She had been so certain that Aunt Sarah would be there, that she had not even wondered what she should do in any other case. Mrs. Forrest had promised to come herself, and Anna could not remember that she had ever failed to carry out her arrangements at exactly the time named.

"If it had been Father, now," she said to herself in her perplexity, "he would perhaps have forgotten, but Aunt Sarah—"

"Any luggage, miss?" asked the red-faced young porter.

"Oh yes, please," said Anna, "and I expected someone to meet me—a lady."

She looked anxiously at him.

"Do'ee want to go into the town?" he asked, as Anna pointed out her trunks. "There's an omnibus outside."

"No, I want to go to Waverley Vicarage," said Anna, feeling very deserted. "How can I get there?"

She followed the porter as he wheeled the boxes outside the station, where a small omnibus was waiting, and also a high spring-cart, in which sat a well-to-do-looking farmer.

"You ain't seen no one from Waverley, Mr. Oswald?" said the porter. "This 'ere young lady expects someone to meet her."

The farmer looked thoughtfully at Anna.

"Waverley, eh," he repeated, "Vicarage?"

"Ah," said the porter, nodding.

Another long gaze.

"Well, I'm going by the gate myself," he said at last. "I reckon Molly wouldn't make much odds of the lot," glancing at the luggage, "if the young lady would like a lift."

"Perhaps," said Anna, hesitatingly, "I'd better have a cab, as Mrs. Forrest is not here."

"I could order you a fly at the Blue Boar," said the porter. "'Twouldn't be ready, not for a half-hour or so. Mr. Oswald 'id get yer over a deal quicker."

No cabs! What a strange place, and how unlike London! Anna glanced uncertainly at the high cart, the tall strawberry horse stamping impatiently, and the good-natured, brown face of the farmer. It would be an odd way of arriving at Waverley, and she was not at all sure that Aunt Sarah would approve of it, but what was she to do? It was very kind of the farmer. Would he expect to be paid?

"Better come along, missie," said Mr. Oswald, as these thoughts passed rapidly through her mind. "You'll be over in a brace of shakes. Hoist them things in at the back, Jim."

Almost before she knew it, Anna had taken the broad hand held out to help her, had mounted the high step, and was seated by the farmer's side.

"Any port in a storm, eh?" he said, good-naturedly, as he put the rug over her knees. "All right at the back, Jim?"

A shake of the reins and Molly dashed forward with a bound that almost threw Anna off her seat and whirled the cart out of the station yard at what seemed to her a fearful pace.

"She'll quiet down directly," said Mr. Oswald. "She's fretted a bit standing at the station. Don't ye be nervous, missie. There's not a morsel of harm in her."

Nevertheless, Anna felt obliged to grasp the side of the cart tightly as Molly turned into the principal street of Dornton, which was wide and, fortunately, nearly empty. What a quiet, dull looking street it was, after the noisy rattle of London, and how low and small the shops and houses looked! If only Molly would go a little slower!

"Yonder's the church," said Mr. Oswald, pointing up a steep side street with his whip, "and yonder's the river," waving it in the opposite direction.

Anna turned her head quickly and caught a hurried glimpse of a gray tower on one side and a thin white streak in the distant, low-lying meadows on the other.

"And here's the new bank," continued Mr. Oswald, with some pride, as they passed a tall, red brick building which seemed to stare the other houses out of countenance, "and the house inside the double white gates is Dr. Hunt's."

"I suppose you know Dornton very well?" Anna said as he paused.

"Been here, man and boy, a matter of forty years—leastways, in the neighborhood," replied the farmer.

"Then you know where Mr. Goodwin lives, I suppose?" said Anna.

"Which of 'em?" said the farmer. "There's Mr. Goodwin, the baker, and Mr. Goodwin, the organist at St. Mary's."

"Oh, the organist," said Anna.

"To be sure I do. He lives in No. 4 Back Row. You can't see it from here. It's an ancient part of Dornton, in between High Street and Market Street. He's been here a sight of years. Everyone knows Mr. Goodwin. He's as well known as the parish church is."

Anna felt pleased to hear that. It convinced her that her grandfather must be an important person, although Back Row did not sound a very important place.

"How fast your horse goes," she said, by way of continuing the conversation, for, after her long silence in the train, it was quite pleasant to talk to somebody.

"Ah, steps out, doesn't she?" said the farmer, with a gratified chuckle. "You won't beat her for pace *this* side of the county. She was bred at Leas Farm, and she's a credit to it."

They were now clear of the town and had turned off the dusty high road into a lane, with hedges on either side.

"Oh, how pretty!" cried Anna.

She could see over these hedges, across the straggling wreaths of dog-roses and clematis, to the meadows on either hand, where the tall grass, sprinkled with silvery ox-eyed daisies, stood ready for hay. Beyond these again came the deep brown of some plowed land, and now and then bits of upland pasture, with cows and sheep feeding. The river Dorn, which Mr. Oswald had pointed out from the town, wound its zigzag course along the valley, which they were now leaving behind them. As they mounted a steep hill, Molly had considerably slackened her speed, so that Anna could look about at her ease and observe all this.

"What a beautiful place this is!" she exclaimed with delight.

"Well enough," said the farmer. "Nice open country. Yonder pasture, where the cows are, belongs to me. If you're stopping at Waverley, missie, I can show you a goodish lot of cows at Leas Farm."

"Oh, I should love to see them!" said Anna.

"My little daughter'll be proud to show 'em yer. She's just twelve years old, Daisy is. Now, you wouldn't guess what I gave her as a birthday present?"

"No," said Anna, "I can't guess at all."

"'Twas as pretty a calf as you ever saw, with a white star on its forehead. Nothing would do after that but I must buy her a collar for it. 'Puppa,' she says, 'when you go into Dornton, you must get me a collar and a bell, like there is in my picture book.' My word!" said the farmer, slapping his knee, "how all the beasts carried on when they first heard that bell in the farmyard! You never saw such antics! It was like as if they were clean mad!"

He threw back his head and gave a jolly laugh at the bare recollection. It was so hearty and full of enjoyment that Anna felt obliged to laugh a little too.

"Here you are, my lass," he said, touching Molly lightly with the whip as they reached the top of the hill. "All level ground now between here and Waverley. Now, what are you shying at?" as Molly swerved away from a stile in the hedge.

It was at an old man who was climbing slowly over it into the steep lane. He wore shabby, black clothes, his shoulders were bent, and his gray hair rather long. In his hand, he carried a violin case.

"That's the Mr. Goodwin you were asking after, missie," said the farmer, touching his hat with his whip as they passed quickly by. "Looks tired, poor old gentleman. Hot day for a long walk."

Anna started and looked eagerly back, but Molly's long stride had already placed a good distance between herself and the figure which was descending the hill. That was her grandfather! Was it possible? He looked so poor, so dusty, so old, such a contrast to the merry June evening, as he tramped wearily down the flowery lane, a little bent to one side by the weight of his violin case. Not an important or remarkable person, such as she had pictured to herself, but a tired old man, of whom the farmer spoke in a tone of pity. Her father had done so too, she remembered. Did everyone pity her grandfather? There was all the more need, certainly, that she should help and cheer him, yet Anna felt vaguely disappointed; she hardly knew why.

These thoughts chased away her smiles completely, and such a grave expression took their place that the farmer noticed the change.

"Tired, missie, eh?" he inquired. "Well, we're there now, so to speak. Yonder's the spire of Waverley church, and the vicarage is close against it—steady then, lass," as Molly objected to turning in at a white gate.

"It's a terrible business traveling by rail," he continued. "Takes the spirit out of you. I'd sooner myself ride on horseback for a whole day than sit in a train half a one."

A long, narrow road, with iron railings on either side, dividing it from broad meadows, brought them to another gate, which the farmer got down to open, and then led Molly up to the porch of the vicarage.

A boy running out from the stableyard close by stood at the horse's head while Mr. Oswald carefully helped Anna down from her high seat, took out her trunks from the back of the cart, and rang the bell. Again the question of payment troubled her, but he did not leave her long to consider it.

"Well, you're landed now, missie," he said with his good-natured smile as he took the reins and turned the impatient Molly towards the gate, "so I'll say good day to you, and my respects to Mr. and Mrs. Forrest."

Molly seemed to Anna to make but one bound from the door to the gate, and to carry the cart and the farmer out of sight, while she was still murmuring her thanks.

She turned to the maid-servant, who had opened the door and was gazing at her and her boxes with some surprise.

"Yes, miss," she said, in answer to Anna's inquiry, "Mrs. Forrest is at home. She's in the garden, if you'll please to come this way. We didn't expect you till tomorrow."

Through the door opposite, Anna could see a lawn, a tea-table under a large tree, a gentleman in a wicker chair, and a lady, in a broad-brimmed hat, sauntering about with a watering pot in her hand. When she saw Anna following the maid, the lady dropped her watering pot and stood rooted to the ground in an attitude of intense surprise.

"Why, Anna!" she exclaimed.

"Didn't you expect me, Aunt Sarah?" said Anna. "Father said you would meet me today."

"Now," said Mrs. Forrest, turning around to her husband in the wicker chair, "isn't that exactly like your brother Bernard?"

"Well, in the meantime, here is Anna, safe and sound," he replied, "so there's no harm done. Come and sit down in the shade, my dear. You've had a hot journey."

"Where's your luggage?" continued Mrs. Forrest, as she kissed her niece. "Did you walk up from the station and leave it there?"

"Oh no, Aunt. I didn't know the way," said Anna.

She began to feel afraid she had done quite the wrong thing in coming with Mr. Oswald.

"Oh, you had to take a fly," said Mrs. Forrest. "It's a most provoking thing altogether."

"It doesn't really matter much, my dear, does it?" said Mr. Forrest as he placed a chair for his niece. "She's managed to get here without any accident, although you did not meet her. Suppose you give us some tea."

"I took the trouble to make a note of the train and day," continued Mrs. Forrest, "and I repeated them twice to Bernard so that there should be no mistake."

"Well, you couldn't have done more," said Mr. Forrest soothingly. "Bernard always was a forgetful fellow, you know."

"Such a very unsuitable thing for the child to arrive quite alone at the station, and no one to meet her there! And I had made all my arrangements for tomorrow so carefully."

As Anna drank her tea, she listened to all this and intended every moment to mention that Mr. Oswald had driven her from the station, but she was held back by a mixture of shyness and fear of what her aunt would say. Perhaps she had done something very silly, and what Mrs. Forrest would call unsuitable! At any rate, it was easier just now to leave her under the impression that she had taken a fly, but, of course, directly if she got a chance, she would tell her all about it. For some time, however, Mrs. Forrest continued to lament that her arrangements had not been properly carried out, and when the conversation did change, Anna had a great many questions to answer about her father and his intended journey. Then a message was brought out to her uncle, over which he and Mrs. Forrest bent in grave consultation. She had now leisure to look about her. How pretty it all was! The long, low front of the vicarage stood facing her, with the smooth green lawn between them, and up the support of the veranda, there were masses of climbing plants in full bloom. The old part of the house had a very deep, red-tiled roof, with little windows poking out of it here and there, and the wing which the present Vicar had built stood at right angles to it. Anna thought her father was right in not admiring the new bit as much as the old, but, nevertheless, with the evening light resting on it, it all looked very pretty and peaceful just now.

"And how do you like the look of Waverley, Anna?" asked Mrs. Forrest.

Anna could answer with great sincerity that she thought it was a lovely place, and she said it so heartily that her aunt was evidently pleased. She kissed her.

"I hope you will be happy whilst you are with us, my dear," she said, "and that Waverley may always be full of pleasant recollections to you."

Anna was wakened the next morning from a very sound sleep by a little tapping noise at her window, which she heard for some time in a sort of half-dream, without being quite roused by it. It was so persistent, however, that at last she felt she must open her eyes to find out what it was. Where was she? For the first few minutes, she looked around the room in puzzled surprise and could not make it out at all. It was so quiet, and clear, and bright, with sunbeams dancing about on the walls, so different altogether from the dingy, gray color of a morning in London. Soon, however, she remembered she was in the country at Waverley, and her mother's picture on the toilet-table brought back to her mind all that had passed yesterday—her journey, her drive with the farmer, her grandfather in the lane.

There were two things she must certainly do today, she told herself as she watched the quivering shadows on the wall. First, she must ask her aunt to let her go at once and see her grandfather, and then she must tell her about her arrival at the station yesterday, and how kindly Farmer Oswald had come to her help. It was strange—now that she had actually got to Waverley, and was only two miles away from her grandfather, she did not feel nearly so eager to talk to him as she had while she was on her journey. However, she need not think about that now. Here she was at Waverley, where it was all sunny and delightful. She should not see smoky London, or have any more walks in the park with her governess, for a long while, perhaps never again. She meant to enjoy herself and be very happy, and nothing disagreeable or tiresome could happen in this beautiful place.

There was the little tapping noise again! What could it be? Anna jumped out of bed, went softly to the window, and drew up the blind. Her bedroom was over the veranda, up which some cluster-roses had climbed, flung themselves in masses on the roof, and reached out some of their branches as far as the window sill. One bold little bunch had pressed itself close up against the pane, and the tight pink buds clattered against it whenever they were stirred by the breeze. The tapping noise was fully accounted for, but Anna could not turn away; it was all so beautiful and so new to her.

She pushed up the window and leaned out. What a lovely smell! There was a long bed of mignonette and heliotrope just below, but, besides the fragrance from this, the air was full of all the sweet scents which belong to an early summer morning in the country. What nice, curious noises, too, all mixed up together! The bees buzzing in the flowers beneath, the little winds rustling in the leaves, the cheerful chirps and scraps of song from the birds, the crow of a distant cock, the deep, low cooing of the pigeons in the stableyard near. Anna longed to be out-of-doors, among these pleasant sights and sounds. She suddenly turned away and began to dress quickly. The stable clock struck seven just as she was ready, and she ran downstairs into the garden with a delightful sense of freedom. The sunshine was splendid! This was indeed different from walking in a London park. How happy she should be in this beautiful place! On exploring a little, she found that the garden was not nearly so large as it looked, for the end of it was hidden by a great walnut tree which stood on the lawn. Behind this came a square piece of kitchen garden, divided from the fields by a sunk fence, with a little wooden footbridge across it.

Anna danced along by the side of the border, where the flowers stood in blooming luxuriance and the most perfect order. Aunt Sarah was justly proud of her garden, and at present, it was in brilliant perfection. Anna knew hardly any of their names, and indeed, except for the roses, they were strange to her. She had not thought there could be so many kinds, and all so beautiful. Reaching the kitchen garden, however, she found some old friends—a long row of sweet peas, fluttering on their stems, like many colored butterflies poised for flight. These were familiar, for she had seen them in greengrocer's shops in London, tied up in tight, close bunches. How different they looked at Waverley! The colors were twice as bright.

"I like these best of all," she said aloud, and as she spoke, a step sounded on the gravel. There was Aunt Sarah in her garden hat, with a basket and scissors in her hand.

"You admire my sweet peas, Anna," she said, kissing her. "I came out to gather some. I find it is so much better to get my flowers before the sun is too hot. Now, you can help me."

They walked slowly along the hedge of sweet peas together, picking them as they went.

"What a beautiful garden yours is, Aunt Sarah," cried Anna.

Mrs. Forrest looked pleased.

"There are many larger ones about here," she said, "but I certainly think my flowers do me credit. I attend to them a great deal myself, but, of course, I cannot give them as much time as I should like. Now you are come, and we shall be busier than ever because we must give some time every day to your studies."

"Miss Milverton said she would write to you about the lessons I have been doing, Aunt," said Anna.

"I have arranged," continued Aunt Sarah, "to read with you for an hour every morning. It is difficult to squeeze it in, but I have managed it. And then I am hoping that you will join in some lessons with the Palmers—girls of your own age, who live near. If their governess will allow you to learn French and German with them, it would be a good plan and would give you companions besides. By the way, Anna, Miss Milverton says in her letter that you don't make any progress in your music. How is that?"

"I don't care very much for music," said Anna. "I would much rather not go on with it, unless you want me to."

She thought that her aunt looked rather relieved, as she

remarked that it was useless for people who were not musical to waste their time in learning to play and that she should not make a point of music lessons at present.

"Now I must cut some roses," added Mrs. Forrest as she put the glowing bunches of sweet peas into her basket. "Come this way."

Anna followed to a little nursery of standard rose trees near the footbridge.

"What are those chimneys I can just see straight over the fields?" she asked her aunt.

"Leas Farm," she replied. "It belongs to Mr. Oswald, a respectable farmer, who owns a good deal of land around here. We have our milk and butter from him. Your uncle used to keep his own cows, but he found them a trouble, and Mrs. Oswald is an excellent dairy woman."

Here was an opportunity for Anna's explanation. The words were on her lips when they were interrupted by the loud sound of a bell from the house.

"The breakfast bell!" said Mrs. Forrest, abruptly turning away from her roses and beginning to hasten towards the house without pausing a moment. "I hope you will always be particular in one point, my dear Anna, and that is punctuality. More hangs upon it than most people recognize—the comfort of a household certainly does. If you are late for one thing, you are late for the next, and so on, until the whole day is thrown into disorder. I am obliged to map my day carefully out to get through my business, and I expect others to do the same. I speak seriously, because your father is one of the most unpunctual men I ever knew, and if you have inherited his failing, you cannot begin to struggle against it too soon."

Anna had not been many days at the vicarage before she found that punctuality was Aunt Sarah's idol and that nothing offended her more than want of respect to it from others. Certainly, everything went like clockwork at Waverley, and though

Anna fancied that Mr. Forrest inwardly rebelled a little, he was outwardly quite submissive. All Aunt Sarah's arrangements and plans were so neatly fitted into each other that the least transgression in one upset the next, and the effect of this was that she had no odds and ends of leisure to spare. Anna even found it difficult to put to her all the questions she had in her mind.

"Not now, my dear, I am engaged," was the frequent reply. She managed to learn, however, that a visit to her grandfather had already been planned for that week and that Mrs. Forrest intended to leave her at his house at Dornton and fetch her again after driving farther on to make a call.

With this she was obliged to be satisfied, and it was quite strange how, after a few days, the new surroundings and rules and pleasures of Waverley seemed to make much that had filled her mind on her arrival fade and grow less important. She still wished to see her grandfather again, but the idea of being his chief comforter and support now seemed impossible, and rather foolish, and she would not have hinted it to Aunt Sarah on any account. Neither did it seem necessary, as the days went on, to mention her drive with Mr. Oswald and the accident of passing her grandfather in the lane.

Chapter 4

The Professor

*I have heard a grave divine say that God has two dwellings—
one in heaven, and the other in a meek and thankful heart.*

IZAAK WALTON

Del, my love," said Mrs. Hunt, "I feel one of my worst headaches coming on. Will you go this afternoon to see Mrs.
Winn, instead of me?"

Delia stood under the medlar tree on the lawn, ready to
go out, with a bunch of roses in her hand and her violin case.
She looked at her mother inquiringly, for Mrs. Hunt had not
just then any appearance of discomfort. She was sitting in an
easy canvas chair, a broad-brimmed hat upon her head and a
newspaper in her hands. Her slippered feet rested on a little
wooden stool, and on a table by her side were a cup of tea, a
nicely buttered roll, and a few very ripe strawberries.

"Hadn't you better wait," said Delia, after a moment's pause,
"until you can go yourself? Mrs. Winn would much rather see
you. Besides—it is my music afternoon."

Mrs. Hunt was looking up and down the columns of the
paper while her daughter spoke. She did not answer at once,
and when she did, it was scarcely an answer so much as a con-
tinuation of her own train of thoughts.

"She has had a tickling cough for so many nights. She can hardly sleep for it, and I promised her a pot of my own black currant jelly."

"It's a great deal out of my way," said Delia.

"If you go," continued Mrs. Hunt, without raising her eyes, "you will find the row of little pots on the top shelf of the store-room cupboard."

Delia bit her lip.

"If I go," she said, "I must shorten my music lesson."

Mrs. Hunt said nothing but looked as amiable as ever. A frown gathered on Delia's forehead. She stood irresolute for a minute and then, with a sudden effort, turned and went quickly into the house. Mrs. Hunt stirred her tea, tasted a strawberry, and leaned back in her chair with a gentle sigh of comfort. In a few minutes, Delia reappeared hurriedly.

"There is *no* black currant jelly in the storeroom," she said with an air of exasperation.

Mrs. Hunt looked up in mild surprise.

"How strange!" she said. "Could I have moved those pots? Ah, now I remember! I had a dream that all the jam was moldy, and so I moved it into the cupboard in the kitchen. That was why Cook left. She didn't like me to use that cupboard for the jam."

"And, meanwhile, where is it?" said Delia.

"Such a wicked mother to give you so much trouble!" murmured Mrs. Hunt with a sweet smile. "But, Del, my love, you must try not to look so morose for trifles. It gives *such* an ugly turn to the features. You'll find the jelly in that nice corner cupboard in the kitchen. Here's the key—" feeling in her pocket, "no, it is not here—where did I leave my keys? Oh, you'll find them in the pocket of my black serge dress, and if they're not there, they are sure to be in the pocket of my gardening apron. My kind love to Mrs. Winn. Tell her to take it constantly in the night. And don't hurry love, it's *so* warm. You look heated already."

In spite of this last advice, it was almost at a run that Delia, having at last found the keys and the jam, set forth on her errand. Perhaps, if she were very quick, she need not lose much time with the Professor, after all, but she felt ruffled and rather cross at the delay. It was not an unusual frame of mind, for she was not naturally of a patient temper, and she did not bear very well the little daily frets and jars of her life. She chafed inwardly as she went quickly on her way, that her music, which seemed to her the most important thing in the world, should be sacrificed to anything so uninteresting and dull as Mrs. Winn's black currant jam. It was all the more trying this afternoon, because, since Anna Forrest's arrival, she had purposely kept away from the Professor and had not seen him for a whole fortnight. A mixed feeling of jealousy and pride had made her determined that Anna should have every opportunity of making Mr. Goodwin's acquaintance without any interference from herself. It was only just and right that his grandchild should have the first place in his affections, the place which hitherto had been her own. Well, now she must take the second place, and if Anna made the Professor happier, it would not matter. At any rate, no one should know, however keenly she felt it.

Mrs. Winn, who was a widow, lived in an old-fashioned, red brick house facing the High Street. It had a respectable, dignified appearance, suggesting solid comfort, like the person of its owner. Mrs. Winn, however, was a lady not anxious for her own well-being only but most charitably disposed towards others who were not so prosperous as herself. She was the vicar's right hand in all the various methods for helping the poor of his parish—clothing clubs, Dorcas meetings, coal clubs, and the lending library—were all indebted to Mrs. Winn for substantial aid, both in the form of money and personal help.

She was looked up to as a power in Dornton, and her house was much frequented by all those interested in parish matters, so that she was seldom to be found alone. Perhaps, also, the fact that the delightful bow window of her usual upstairs sitting

room looked straight across to Appleby's, the post office and
stationer, increased its attractions. "It makes it so lively," Mrs.
Winn was wont to observe. "I seldom pass a day, even if I don't
go out, without seeing Mr. Field, or Mr. Hurst, or some of the
country clergy, going in and out of Appleby's. I never feel dull."

Today, to her great relief, Delia found Mrs. Winn quite
alone. She was sitting at a table drawn up into the bow window,
busily engaged in covering books with whitey-brown paper.
On her right was a pile of gaily bound volumes, blue, red, and
purple, which were quickly reduced to a pale brown, unat-
tractive appearance in her practiced hands, and placed in a pile
on her left. Delia thought Mrs. Winn looked as whitey-brown
as the books, for there was no decided color about her. Her
eyes were pale, as well as the narrow line of hair which showed
beneath the border of her white cap, and her dresses were
always of a doubtful shade, between brown and gray.

She welcomed Delia kindly, but with the repressed air of
severity which she always reserved for her.

"How like your dear mother!" she exclaimed on receiving
the pot of jelly. "Yes, my cough is a little better, tell her, but I
thought I would keep indoors today, and, you see, I've all these
books to get through, so it's just as well. Mr. Field got them in
London for the library the other day."

"What a pity they must be covered," said Delia, glancing
from one pile to the other. "The children would like the bright
colors so much better."

"A nice state they would be in, in a week," said Mrs. Winn
stolidly as she folded, and snipped, and turned a book about
in her large, capable hands. "Besides, it's better to teach the
children not to care for pretty things."

"Is it?" said Delia. "I should have thought that was just
what they ought to learn."

"The love of pretty things," said Mrs. Winn, sternly, "is
like the love of money, the root of all evil, and it has led quite
as many people astray. All these books have to be labeled and

numbered," she added, after a pause. "You might do some, Delia, if you're not in a hurry."

"Oh, but I am," said Delia, glancing at the clock. "I am going to Mr. Goodwin for a lesson, and I am late already."

Mrs. Winn had, however, some information to give about Mr. Goodwin. Julia Gibbins, who had just looked in, had met him on the way to give a lesson at Pynes.

"So," she added, "he can't possibly be home for another half-hour at least, you know, and you may just as well spend the time in doing something useful."

With a little sigh of disappointment, Delia took off her gloves and seated herself opposite to Mrs. Winn. Everything seemed against her today.

"And how," said that lady, having supplied her with scissors and paper, "do you get on with Anna Forrest? You're with Mr. Goodwin so much, I suppose you know her quite well by this time."

"Indeed, I don't," said Delia. "I haven't even seen her yet, have you?"

"I've seen her twice," said Mrs. Winn. "She's pretty enough, though not to be compared to her mother; more like the Forrests, and she has her father's pleasant manners. If *looks* were the only things to consider, she would do very well."

"What's the matter with her?" asked Delia, bluntly, for Mrs. Winn spoke as though she knew much more than she expressed.

"Why, I've every reason to suppose—" she began deliberately, then breaking off. "Take care, Delia," she exclaimed. "You're cutting that cover too narrow. Let me show you. You must leave a good bit to tuck under, don't you see, or it will be off again directly."

Delia had never in her life been so anxious for Mrs. Winn to finish a sentence, but she tried to control her impatience and bent her attention to the brown paper cover.

"It only shows," continued Mrs. Winn, when her instruc-
tions were ended, "that I was right in what I said the other day
about Mr. Bernard Forrest's marriage. That sort of thing never
answers. That child has evidently been brought up without a
strict regard for truth."

"What has she done?" asked Delia.

"Not, of course," said Mrs. Winn, "that poor Prissy could
have had anything to do with that."

The book Delia held slipped from her impatient fingers and
fell to the ground flat on its face.

"My *dear* Delia," said Mrs. Winn, picking it up and
smoothing the leaves, with a shocked look, "the books get
worn out quite soon enough without being tossed about like
that."

"I'm very sorry," said Delia humbly, "but do tell me what it
is you mean about Anna Forrest."

"It's nothing at all pleasant," said Mrs. Winn, "but as you're
likely to see something of her, you ought to know that I've
every reason to believe that she's not quite straightforward.
Now, with all your faults, Delia—and you've plenty of them—I
never found you untruthful."

She fixed her large, round eyes on her companion for a
moment, but as Delia made no remark, she resumed—

"On the evening of your last working party but one, Julia
Gibbins and I saw Mr. Oswald of Leas Farm driving Anna
Forrest from the station. Of course, we didn't know her then.
But Julia felt sure it was Anna, and it turned out she was right.
Curiously enough, we met Mrs. Forrest and the child in Appleby's shortly after, and Mrs. Forrest said how unlucky it had
been that there was a confusion about the day of her niece's
arrival, and no one was there to meet her at the station; but,
fortunately, she said, Anna was sensible enough to take a fly, so
that was all right. Now, you see, my dear Delia, she *didn't* take
a fly," added Mrs. Winn solemnly, "so she must have deceived
her aunt."

Mrs. Winn's most important stories had so often turned out

to be founded on mistakes that Delia was not much impressed by this one, nor disposed to think worse of Anna because of it.

"Oh, I daresay there's a mistake somewhere," she said lightly, rising and picking up her flowers and her violin case. "I must go now, Mrs. Winn. The Professor will be back by the time I get there. Goodbye."

She hurried out of the room before Mrs. Winn could begin another sentence, for long experience had taught her that the subject would not be exhausted for a long while and that a sudden departure was the only way of escape.

A quarter of an hour's quick walk brought her to No. 4 Back Row, and looking in at the sitting room window, as her custom was, she saw that the Professor had indeed arrived before her.

His dwelling was a contrast in every way to that of Mrs. Winn. For one thing, instead of standing boldly out before the world of Dornton High Street, it was smuggled away, with a row of little houses like itself, in a narrow sort of passage, enclosed between two wide streets. This passage ended in a blank wall, and was, besides, too narrow for any but foot passengers to pass up it, so that it would have been hard to find a quieter or more retired spot. The little old houses in it were only one story high, and very solidly built, with thick walls, and the windows in deep recesses. Before each, a strip of garden and a gravel walk stretched down to a small gate. Back Row was the very oldest part of Dornton, and though the houses were small, they had always been lived in by respectable people and preserved a certain air of gentility.

Without waiting to knock, Delia hurried in at the door of No. 4, which led straight into the sitting room. The Professor was leaning back in his easy chair, his boots white with dust, and an expression of fatigue and dejection over his whole person.

"Oh, Professor," was her first remark, as she threw down her violin case, "you *do* look tired! Have you had your tea?"

"I believe, my dear," he replied, rather faintly, "Mrs. Cooper has not come in yet."

Mrs. Cooper was a charwoman, who came in at uncertain intervals to cook the Professor's meals and clean his rooms. As he was not exacting, the claims of her other employers were always satisfied first, and if she were at all busier than usual, he often got scanty attention.

Without waiting to hear more, Delia made her way to the little kitchen and set about her preparations in a very businesslike manner. She was evidently well acquainted with the resources of the household, for she bustled about, opening cupboards and setting tea things on a tray, as though she were quite at home. In a wonderfully short time, she had prepared a tempting meal and carried it into the sitting room, so that, when the Professor came back from changing his boots, he found everything quite ready. His little round table, cleared of the litter of manuscripts and music books, was drawn up to the window and covered with a white cloth. On it there was some steaming coffee, eggs, and bread and butter, a bunch of roses in the middle, and his armchair placed before it invitingly.

He sank into it with a sigh of comfort and relief.

"How very good your coffee smells, Delia!" he said. "Quite different from Mrs. Cooper's."

"I daresay, if the truth were known," said Delia, carefully pouring it out, "that you had no dinner to speak of before you walked up to Pynes and back again."

"I had a sandwich," answered Mr. Goodwin meekly, for Delia was bending a searching and severe look upon him.

"Then Mrs. Cooper didn't come!" she exclaimed. "Really, we ought to look out for someone else. I believe she does it on purpose."

"Now I beg of you, Delia," said the Professor, leaning forward earnestly, "not to send Mrs. Cooper away. She's a very poor woman and would miss the money. She told me only the last time she was here that the doctor had ordered cod-liver oil for the twins, and she couldn't afford to give it to them."

"Oh, the twins!" said Delia, with a little scorn.

"Well, my dear, she *has* twins. She brought them here once in a perambulator."

"But that's no reason at all she should not attend properly to you," said Delia.

Mr. Goodwin put down his cup of coffee, which he had begun to drink with great relish, and looked thoroughly cast down.

Delia laughed a little.

"Well, I won't, then," she said. "Mrs. Cooper shall stay, and neglect her duties, and spoil your food, as long as you like."

"Thank you, my dear," said the Professor, brightening up again. "She really does extremely well; though, of course, she doesn't," glancing at the table, "make things look so nice as you do."

Delia blamed herself for staying away so long when she saw with what contented relish her old friend had applied himself to the simple fare she had prepared. It made her thoroughly ashamed to think that he should have suffered neglect through her small feelings of jealousy and pride. He should not be left for a whole fortnight again to Mrs. Cooper's tender mercies.

"We are to have a lesson tonight, I hope," said Mr. Goodwin presently. "It must be a long time since we had one, Delia, isn't it?"

"A whole fortnight," she answered, "but," glancing wistfully at her violin case, "you've had such hard work today, I know, if you've been to Pynes. Perhaps it would be better to put it off."

But Mr. Goodwin would not hear of this. It would refresh him. It would put the other lessons out of his head. They would try over the last sonata he had given Delia to practice.

"Did you make anything of it?" he asked. "It is rather difficult."

Delia's face, which until now had been full of smiles and happiness, clouded over mournfully.

"Oh, Professor," she cried, "I'm in despair about my practicing. If I could get some more clear time to it, I know I could get on. But it's always the same; the days get frittered up into tiny bits with things which don't seem to matter, and I feel I don't make any progress. Just as I am getting a hard passage right, I have to break off."

This was evidently not a new complaint to Mr. Goodwin.

"Well, well, my dear," he said kindly. "We will try it over together and see how we get on. I daresay it is better than you think."

Delia quickly collected the tea things and carried them into the kitchen to prevent any chance of Mrs. Cooper clattering and banging about the room during the lesson. Then she took out her violin, put her music on the stand, and began to play without more ado. The Professor leaned back in his chair meanwhile, with closed eyes, and ears on the alert to detect faults or passages wrongly rendered. As he sat there, perfectly still, a calm expression came into his face, which made him for the time look much younger than was usually the case. He was not a very old man, but past troubles had left their traces in deep lines and wrinkles, and his hair was quite white. Only his eyes preserved that look of eternal youth which is sometimes granted to those whose thoughts have always been unselfish, kindly, and generous. Delia played on, halting a little over difficult passages, and as she played the Professor's face changed with the music, showing sometimes an agony of anxiety during an intricate bit and relaxing into a calm smile when she got to smooth water again.

Once, as though urged by some sudden impulse, he rose and began to stride up and down the room, but when she saw this, Delia dropped her bow and said in a warning voice, "Now, Professor!" when he at once resumed his seat and waited patiently until she had finished.

"It won't do, Delia," he said. "You've got the idea, but you can't carry it out."

"Oh, I know," she replied mournfully. "I know how bad it is, and the worst of it is that I can hear how it ought to be all the time."

"No," he said quickly, "that's not the worst of it. That's the best of it. If you were satisfied with it as it is, you would be a hopeless pupil. But you've something of the true artist in you, Delia. The true artist, you know, is never satisfied."

"I believe, though," said Delia, "that if I could shut myself up alone somewhere for a time with my violin, and no one to disturb me, I should be able to do something. I might not be satisfied, but oh, how happy I should be! As it is—"

"As it is, you must do as greater souls have done before you," put in the Professor, "and win your way towards your ideal through troubles and hindrances."

"I don't get far, though," said Delia mournfully.

"Do you think you would get far by shutting yourself away from the common duties of your life?" said Mr. Goodwin in a kind voice. "It's a very poor sort of talent that wants petting and coaxing like that. Those great souls in the past who have taught us most have done it while reaching painfully up to their vision through much that thwarted and baffled them. Their lives teach us as well as their art, and believe me, Delia, when the artist's life fails in duty and devotion, his art fails, too, in some way."

"It is so hard to remember that all those dusty, little, every-day things matter," said Delia.

"But if you think of what they stand for, they do matter very much. Call them self-discipline, and patience, and they are very important, above all, to an artist. I have heard people say," continued Mr. Goodwin reflectively, "that certain failings of temper and self-control are to be excused in artists because their natures are sensitive. Now, that seems to me the very reason that they should be better than other people—more open to good influences. And I believe, when this has not been so, it has been owing rather to a smallness of character than to their artistic temperament."

Delia smiled.

"I don't know," she said, "if I have anything of an artist in me, but I have a small character, for I am always losing my temper—except when I am with you, Professor. If I talked to you every day, and had plenty of time to practice, I should have the good temper of an angel."

"But not of a human being. That must come, not from outward things being pleasant, but from inward things being right. Believe an old man, my dear, who has had some trials and disappointments in his life, the best sort of happiness is his—

> 'Whose high endeavors are an inward light
> Which makes the path before him always bright.'

"Those endeavors may not bring fame or success, but they do bring light to shine on all those everyday things you call dusty and turn them to gold."

Delia stood by her music stand, her eyes fixed on the window and a rebellious little frown on her brow.

"But I should *love* to be famous," she suddenly exclaimed, reaching up her arms and clasping her hands behind her head. "Professor, I should *love* it! Fancy being able to play so as to speak to thousands of people and make them hear what you say; to make them glad one moment and sorry the next; to have it in your power to move a whole crowd, as some musicians have! It must be a splendid life. Shouldn't *you* like it?"

Mr. Goodwin's glance rested on his enthusiastic pupil with a little amusement.

"It's rather late in the day for me to consider the question, isn't it?" he said.

"Didn't you ever want to go away from Dornton and play to people who understand what you mean?" asked Delia impatiently. "Instead of playing the organ in St. Mary's and teaching me, you might be a famous musician in London, with crowds of people flocking to hear you."

"Perhaps," said the Professor quietly, "who knows?"

"Then," she continued, dropping her arms and turning to him with sudden determination, "then, oh Professor, why *didn't* you go?"

The question had been in her mind a very long time. Now it was out, and she was almost frightened by her own rashness. Mr. Goodwin, however, seemed neither surprised nor annoyed.

"Well, Delia," he answered with a gentle shake of the head, "I suppose two things have kept me in Dornton—two very strong things—poverty and pride. I had my chance once, but it came in a shape I couldn't bring myself to accept. 'There is a tide in the affairs of men,' you know, and if one neglects it—"

He broke off and bent over his violin, which he had taken up from the ground.

"Of course," said Delia, looking at him with great affection, "I'm glad you didn't go, for my own sake. You and music make Dornton bearable."

"You always speak so disdainfully of poor Dornton," said Mr. Goodwin, drawing his bow softly across his violin. "Now, I've known it longer than you, and really, when I look back, I've been very happy. Dornton has given me the best any place has to give—people to love and care for. After Prissy's marriage there were some lonely days, to be sure. I could not feel very happy about that, for she seemed to be taken out of my life altogether, and there came sadder days still when she died. You were only a little toddling child then, Delia, and yet it seemed a short while before we began to be friends, and," holding out his hand to her, "we've been friends ever since, haven't we? So, you see, I ought not to be ungrateful to Dornton."

"And now," added Delia with an effort, "there is Anna, your grandchild. Perhaps you will make her famous, though you wouldn't be famous yourself."

Mr. Goodwin shook his head.

"Anna will never be famous in that way," he said. "She has a sweet, affectionate manner, but there's nothing that reminds me of her mother at all, or of our family. It's quite an effort to realize that she is Prissy's child. It's a very curious feeling."

"Have you seen her often?" asked Delia.

"Only twice. I don't at all suppose, as matters stand, that I shall ever see much of her. I am so busy, you see, and she tells me her aunt has all sorts of plans for her—lessons and so on."

"But," said Delia rather indignantly, "she *ought* to come and see you often."

"I shall not complain if she doesn't, and I shall not be surprised. There was a matter, years ago, in which I differed from Mrs. Forrest, and I have never been to Waverley since. We are quite friendly when we meet, but there can never be really cordial relations between us."

"If I were Anna—" began Delia impetuously.

"But you are *not* Anna," interrupted Mr. Goodwin with a smile. "You are Delia Hunt, and you are made of different materials. If I am not mistaken, Anna is affectionate and yielding and will be influenced by those she is with. And then she's very young, you see. She could not oppose her aunt and uncle, and I'm sure I do not wish it. I shall not interfere with her life at Waverley. The Forrests are kind people, and I feel sure she will be very happy there. She will do very well without me."

He turned towards his pupil and added, rather wistfully, "I should like *you* to be friends with her, though, Delia. It would be a comfort to me."

"Indeed, I will try my best, Professor," she exclaimed earnestly. Her jealousy of Anna seemed very small and mean, and she felt anxious to atone for it.

"That's good," said Mr. Goodwin, with a contented air. "I know you will do what you promise. Now it's my turn to play the sonata and yours to listen."

As the first plaintive notes of the violin filled the little room, Delia threw herself into the window seat, leaned back her head, and gave herself up to the enjoyment.

The Professor's playing meant many things to her. It meant a journey into another country where all good and noble things were possible, where vexations and petty cares could not enter, nor anything that thwarted and baffled. It meant a sure refuge for a while from the small details of her life in Dornton, which she sometimes found so wearisome. The warning tones of the church clock checked her flight through these happy regions and brought her down to earth just as the Professor's last note died away.

"Oh, how late it is!" she exclaimed as she started up and put on her hat. "Goodbye, Professor. Oh, if I could only make it speak like that!"

"Patience, patience," he said with his kind smile. "We all hear and see better things than we can express, you know, but that will come to us all someday."

Chapter 5
Anna Makes Friends

*Sweet language will multiply friends: and a fair-speaking
tongue will increase kind greetings.*

ECCLESIASTICUS

Delia kept her promise in mind through all the various duties and occupations of the next few days and wondered how she could carry it out. She began, apart from the wish to please the Professor, to have a great desire to know Anna for her own sake. Would they be friends? And what sort of girl was she? Mr. Goodwin had told her so very little. Affectionate, sweet-tempered, yielding, she might be all that without being very interesting. Still, she hoped they might be able to like each other, for although the Hunts had a wide acquaintance, Delia had few friends of her own age, nor anyone with whom she felt in entire sympathy, except the Professor. Delia was not popular in Dornton, and people regretted that such a "sweet" woman as Mrs. Hunt should have a daughter who was often so blunt in her manners and so indisposed to make herself pleasant. Her life, therefore, though full of busy matters, was rather lonely; and she would have made it still more so, if possible, by shutting herself up with her violin and her books. The bustling sociabilities of her home, however, prevented this; and she was constantly obliged, with inward revolt, to leave the things she loved for some social occasion or to pick up the dropped stitches of Mrs. Hunt's household affairs.

There were endless little matters from morning till night for Delia to attend to, and it was only by getting up very early that she found any time at all for her studies and her music. In winter this was hard work, and progress with her violin was almost impossible for stiff, cold fingers. But no one at her home took Delia's music seriously. It was an accomplishment, a harmless amusement, but by no means to be allowed to take time from more important affairs. It did not matter whether she practiced or not, but it did matter that she should be ready to make calls with her mother or to carry soup to someone in Mrs. Hunt's district who had been overlooked. She would have given up her music altogether if her courage had not been revived from time to time by Mr. Goodwin, and her ambition rekindled by hearing him play. As it was, she always came back to it with fresh heart and hope after seeing him.

For nearly a week after her last visit, Delia awoke every morning with a determination to walk over to Waverley, and each day passed without her having done so. At last, however, chance arranged her meeting with Anna. Coming into the drawing room one afternoon in search of her mother, she found not Mrs. Hunt but a tall girl of fourteen, with light yellow hair, sitting in the window with a patient expression, as though she had been waiting there some time. Delia advanced uncertainly. She knew who it was. There was only one stranger likely to appear just now. It must be Anna Forrest. But it was so odd to find her there, just when she had been thinking of her so much, that for a moment she hardly knew what to say.

The girl, however, was quite at her ease.

"I am Anna Forrest," she said. "Mrs. Hunt asked me to come in, then she went to find you. You are Delia, are you not?"

She had a bright, frank manner, with an entire absence of shyness, which attracted Delia immediately. She found, on inquiry, that Mrs. Hunt had met Anna in the town with her aunt and had asked her to come in. Mrs. Forrest had driven home, and Anna was to walk back after tea.

"And have you been waiting long?" asked Delia.

"It must have been an hour, I think," said Anna, "because I heard the church clock. But it hasn't seemed long," she added hastily. "I've been looking out at the pigeons in the garden."

Delia felt no doubt whatever that Mrs. Hunt had been called off in some other direction and had completely forgotten her guest. However, here was Anna at last.

"Come upstairs and take off your hat in my room," she said.

Delia's room was at the top of the house—a garret with a window looking across the red-tiled roofs of the town to the distant meadows, through which glistened the crooked silver line of the River Dorn. She was fond of standing at this window in her few idle moments, with her arms crossed on the high ledge and her gaze directed far away. To it were confided all the hopes and wishes and dreams which were, as a rule, carefully locked up in her own breast, and of which only one person in Dornton even guessed the existence.

Anna glanced curiously around as she entered. The room had rather a bare look, after the bright prettiness of Waverley, though it contained all Delia's most cherished possessions—a shelf of books, a battered old brown desk, her music stand, and her violin.

"Oh," she exclaimed as her eye fell on the last, "can you play the violin? Will you play to me?"

Delia hesitated. She was not fond of playing to people who did not care for music, though she was often obliged to do so, but Anna pressed her so earnestly that she did not like to be ungracious; and, taking up her violin, she played a short German air, which she thought might please her visitor.

Anna, meanwhile, paid more attention to her new acquaintance than to her performance and looked at her with great interest. There was something about Delia's short, compact figure; her firm chin; the crisp, wavy hair which rose from her broad, low forehead like a sort of halo, which gave an impression of strength and reliability not unmingled with self-will. This last quality, however, was not so marked while she was playing. Her face then was at its best, and its usual somewhat defiant air softened into a wishfulness which was almost beauty. Before the tune was finished, Anna was quite ready to rush into a close friendship, if Delia would respond to it, but of this she felt rather in doubt.

"How beautifully you play!" she exclaimed as Delia dropped her bow and shut up her music book.

A very little smile curled Delia's lips.

"That shows one thing," she answered. "You don't know much about music, or you would not call my playing beautiful."

"Well, it sounds so to me," said Anna, a little abashed by this directness of speech, "but I certainly don't know much about music. Aunt Sarah says I need not go on with it while I am here."

"I play very badly," said Delia. "If you wish to hear beautiful playing, you must listen to your grandfather."

"Must I?" said Anna vaguely. "I thought," she added, "that he played the organ in Dornton church."

"So he does," said Delia, "but he plays the violin, too. And he gives lessons. He taught me."

She looked searchingly at her companion, whose fair face reddened a little.

"I owe everything to him," continued Delia. "Without what he has done for me, my life would be dark. He brought light into it when he taught me to play and to love music."

"Did he?" said Anna wonderingly.

She began to feel that she did not understand Delia. She was speaking a strange language, which evidently meant something to her, for her eyes sparkled and her brown cheeks glowed with excitement.

"We ought to be proud in Dornton," Delia went on, "to have your grandfather living here, but we're not worthy of him. His genius would place him in a high position among people who could understand him. Here it's just taken for granted."

Anna grew more puzzled and surprised still. Delia's tone upset the idea she began to have that her grandfather was a person to be pitied. This was a different way of speaking of him, and it was impossible to get used to it all at once. At Waverley he was hardly mentioned at all, and she had come to avoid doing so also, from a feeling that her aunt disliked it. She could not suddenly bring herself to look upon him as a genius, and be proud of him, though she had every wish to please Delia.

"What a pity," she said hesitatingly, "that he is so poor, and has to live in such a very little house, if he is so clever!"

"Poor?" exclaimed Delia indignantly, then, checking herself, she added quietly, "It depends on what you call poor. What the Professor possesses is worth all the silver and gold and big houses in the world. And that's just what the Dornton people don't understand. Why, the rich ones actually *patronize* him and think he is fortunate in giving their children music lessons."

Delia began to look so wrathful as she went on that Anna longed to change the subject to one which might be more soothing. She could not at all understand why her companion was so angry. It was certainly a pity that Mr. Goodwin was obliged to give lessons, but if he must, it was surely a good thing that people were willing to employ him. While she was pondering this in silence, she was relieved by a welcome proposal from Delia that they should go downstairs and have tea in the garden. "Afterwards," she added, "I will show you the way to Waverley over the fields."

In the garden it was pleasant and peaceful enough. Tea was ready under the shade of the medlar tree. The pigeons whirled and fluttered about over the red roofs all around, settling sometimes on the lawn for a few moments, bowing and cooing to each other. Mrs. Hunt, meanwhile, chatted on in a comfortable way, hardly settling longer on one spot in her talk than the pigeons. From the affairs of her district to the affairs of nature, from an anecdote about the rector to a recipe for scones, she rambled gently on. But at last, coming to a favorite topic, she made a longer rest. Anna was glad of it, for it dealt with people of whom she had been wishing to hear—her mother and her grandfather. Mrs. Hunt had much to tell of the former, whom she had known from the time when she had been a girl of Anna's age until her marriage with Mr. Bernard Forrest. She became quite enthusiastic as one recollection after the other followed.

"A sweeter face and a sweeter character than Prissy Goodwin's could not be imagined," she said. "We were all sorry when she left Dornton, and everyone felt for Mr. Goodwin. Poor man, he's aged a great deal during the last few years. I remember him as upright as a dart and always in good spirits!"

"I have a portrait of my mother," said Anna, "a miniature, painted just after her marriage. It's very pretty indeed."

"It should be, if it's a good likeness," said Mrs. Hunt. "There's never been such a pretty girl in Dornton since your mother went away. I should like to see that portrait. When you come over again, which I hope will be soon, you must bring it with you, and then we will have some more talk about your dear mother."

Anna readily promised, and as she walked up the High Street by Delia's side, her mind was full of all that she had heard that afternoon. It had interested and pleased her very much, but somehow it was difficult to connect Mr. Goodwin and his dusty little house with the picture formed in her mind of her beautiful mother. If only she were alive now!

"I suppose you were a baby when my mother married," she said, suddenly turning to her companion.

"I was two years old," replied Delia, smiling, "but though

I can't remember your mother, I can remember your grandfather when I was quite a little girl. He was always so good to
me. Long before he began to teach me to play, I used to toddle
by his side to church and wait there while he practiced on the
organ. I think it was that which made me first love music."

"It seems so odd," said Anna hesitatingly, "that I should be
his grandchild, and yet that he should be almost a stranger to
me, while you—"

"But," put in Delia quickly, for she thought that Anna was
naturally feeling jealous, "you won't be strangers long now.
You will come over often, and soon you will feel as though
you'd known him always. To tell you the truth," she added
lightly, "I felt dreadfully jealous of you when I first heard you
were coming."

Jealous! How strange that sounded to Anna. She glanced
quickly at her companion and saw that she was evidently in
earnest.

"I don't know, I'm sure, about coming to Dornton often,"
she said, "because, you see, Aunt Sarah is so tremendously
busy, and she likes to do certain things on certain days; but, of
course, I shall come as often as I can. I do hope," she added earnestly, "I shall be able to see you sometimes and that you will
often come over to Waverley."

Delia was silent.

"You see," continued Anna, "I like being at Waverley very
much, and they're very kind indeed; but it *is* a little lonely, and
if you don't mind, I should be *so* glad to have you for a friend."

She turned to her companion with a bright blush and an
appealing look that was almost humble. Delia was touched.
She had begun to think Anna rather cold and indifferent in
the way she had talked about coming to Dornton; but, after all,
it was unreasonable to expect her to feel warm affection for a
grandfather who was almost a stranger. When she knew him,
she would not be able to help loving him, and, meanwhile, she
herself must not forget that she had promised the Professor

to be Anna's friend. No doubt she had said truly that she was lonely at Waverley. She met Anna's advances cordially, therefore, and by the time they had turned off the high road into the fields, the two girls were chatting gaily and were quite at their ease with each other. Everything in this field walk was new and delightful to Anna, and her pleasure increased by feeling that she had made a friend of her own age. The commonest wildflowers on her path were wonderful to her unaccustomed eyes. Delia must tell their names. She must stop to pick some. They were prettier even than Aunt Sarah's flowers at Waverley. What were those growing in the hedge? She ran about admiring and exclaiming until, near the end of the last field, the outbuildings of Leas Farm came in sight, which stood in a lane dividing the farmer's property from Mr. Forrest's.

"There's Mr. Oswald," said Delia suddenly.

Anna looked up. Across the field towards them, mounted on a stout, grey cob, came the farmer at a slow jog-trot. So much had happened since her arrival at Waverley that she had almost forgotten the events of that first evening, and all ideas of telling her aunt of her acquaintance with Mr. Oswald had passed from her mind. As he stopped to greet the girls, however, and make a few leisurely remarks about the weather, it all came freshly to her memory.

"Not been over to see my cows yet, missie," he said, checking his pony again, after he had started, and leaning back in his saddle. "My Daisy's been looking for you every day. You'd be more welcome than ever, now I know who 'twas I had the pleasure of driving the other day—for your mother's sake, as well as your own."

Delia turned an inquiring glance on her companion as they continued their way. Would she say anything? Recollecting Mrs. Winn's story, she rather hoped she would. But Anna, her gay spirits quite checked, walked soberly in perfect silence. It made her uncomfortable to remember that she had never undeceived Aunt Sarah about that fly. What a stupid little mistake it had been! Nothing wrong in what she had done at all, if she had only been quite open about it. What would Delia think of it, she wondered. She glanced sideways at her. What a very firm, decided mouth and chin she had. She looked as though she were never afraid of anything and always quite sure to do right. Perhaps, if she knew of this, she would look as scornful and angry as she had that afternoon, in speaking of the Dornton people. That would be dreadful. Anna could not risk that. She wanted Delia to like and admire her very much, and on no account to think badly of her. So she checked the faint impulse she had had towards the confession of her foolishness and was almost relieved when they reached the point where Delia was to turn back to Dornton. They parted affectionately, with many hopes and promises as to their meeting again soon, and Anna stood at the white gate watching her new friend until she was out of sight.

Then she looked around her. She was in quite a strange land, for although she had now been some weeks at Waverley, she had not yet explored the fields between the village and Dornton. On her right, a little way down the grassy land, stood Mr. Oswald's house, a solid, square building of old, red brick, pleasantly surrounded by barns, cattle sheds, and outbuildings, all of a substantial, prosperous appearance. It crossed Anna's mind that she should very much like to see the farmer's cows, as he had proposed, but she had not the courage to present herself at the house and ask for Daisy. She must content herself by looking in at the farmyard gate as she passed it. A little farther on, Delia had pointed out another gate, on the other side of the lane, which led straight into the vicarage field, and towards this she now made her way.

She was unusually thoughtful as she sauntered slowly down the lane, for her visit to Dornton had brought back thoughts of her mother and grandfather, which had lately been kept in the background. She had today heard them spoken of with affection and admiration, instead of being passed over in silence.

Waverley was very pleasant, Aunt Sarah was kind, and her Uncle John indulgent, but about her relations in Dornton there was scarcely a word spoken. It was strange. She remembered Delia's sparkling eyes as she talked of Mr. Goodwin. That was stranger still. In the two visits Anna had paid to him, she had not discovered much to admire, and she had not been pleased with the appearance of No. 4 Back Row. It had seemed to her then that people called him "poor Mr. Goodwin" with reason: he was poor, evidently, or he would not live all alone in such a very little house, with no servants, and work so hard, and get so tired and dusty as he had looked on that first evening she had seen him. Yet, perhaps, when she knew him as well as Delia did, she should be able to feel proud of him; and, at any rate, he stood in need of love and attention.

She felt drawn to the Hunts and the Dornton people, who had known and loved her mother, and she resolved to make more efforts to go there frequently and to risk displeasing Aunt Sarah and upsetting her arrangements. It would be very disagreeable, for she knew well that neither Mr. Goodwin nor Dornton were favorite subjects at Waverley. When things were going smoothly and pleasantly, it was so much nicer to leave them alone. However, she would try, and just then arriving at the farmyard gate, she dismissed those tiresome thoughts and leaned over to look with great interest at the creatures within. As she did so, a little girl came out of the farmhouse and came slowly down the lane towards her. She was about twelve years old, very childish-looking for her age, and dressed in a fresh, yellow cotton frock, nearly covered by a big, white pinafore. Her little, round head was bare, and her black hair closely cropped like a boy's. She came on with very careful steps, her whole attention fixed on a plate she held firmly with both hands, which had a mug on it full of something she was evidently afraid to spill. Her eyes were so closely bent on this that until she was near Anna she did not see her; and then, with a start, she came suddenly to a standstill, not forgetting to preserve the balance of the mug and plate. It was a very nice, open, little face she raised towards Anna, with a childish and innocent expression, peppered thickly with freckles like a bird's egg, especially over the blunt, round nose.

"Did you come from the vicarage?" she inquired gravely.

"I'm staying there," replied Anna, "but I came over the fields just now from Dornton."

"Those are Puppa's fields," said the child, "and this is Puppa's farm."

"You are Daisy Oswald, I suppose?" said Anna. "Your father asked me to come and see your cows." The little girl nodded.

"I know what your name is," she said. "You're Miss Anna Forrest. Puppa fetched you over from the station. You came quick. Puppa was driving Strawberry Molly that day. No one can do it as quick as her." Then, with a critical glance, "I can ride her. Can you ride?"

"No, indeed, I can't," replied Anna. "But won't you show me your cows?"

"Why, it isn't milking time!" said Daisy lifting her brows with a little surprise. "They're all out in the field." She considered Anna thoughtfully for a moment, and then added, jerking her head towards the next gate, "Won't you come and sit on that gate? I often sit on that gate. Most every evening."

The invitation was made with so much friendliness that Anna could not refuse it.

"I can't stay long," she said, "but I don't mind a little while."

Arrived at the gate, Daisy pushed mug and plate into Anna's hands.

"Hold 'em a minute," she said as she climbed nimbly up and disposed herself comfortably on the top bar. "Now," smoothing her pinafore tightly over her knees, "give 'em to me and come up and sit alongside, and we'll have 'em together. That'll be fine."

Anna was by no means so active and neat in her movements as her companion, for she was not used to climbing gates, but after some struggles, watched by Daisy with a chuckle of amusement, she succeeded in placing herself at her side. In this position they sat facing the vicarage garden at the end of the field. It looked quite near, and Anna hoped that Aunt Sarah might not happen to come this way just at present.

"How nice it is to sit on a gate!" she said. "I never climbed a gate before."

Daisy stared.

"Never climbed a gate before!" she repeated. "Why ever not?"

"Well, you see, I've always lived in a town," said Anna, "where you don't need to climb gates."

Daisy nodded.

"I know," she said, "like Dornton. Now there's two lots of bread and butter, one for me and one for you, and we must take turns to drink. You first."

"But I've had tea, thank you," said Anna. "I won't take any of yours."

Daisy looked a little cast down at this refusal, but she soon set to work heartily on her simple meal alone, stopping in the intervals of her bites and sups to ask and answer questions.

"Was the town you lived in *nicer* than Dornton?" she asked.

"It was not a bit like it," replied Anna. "Much, much larger. And always full of carts, and carriages, and people."

"My!" exclaimed Daisy. "Any shops?"

"Lots and lots. And at night, when they were all lighted up, and the lamps in the streets too, it was as light as day."

"That must have been fine," said Daisy. "I like shops. Were you sorry to come away?"

Anna shook her head.

"Do you like being at Waverley?" pursued the inquiring Daisy, tilting up the mug so that her brown eyes came just above the rim. "There's no one to play with there, but I s'pose you don't mind. I haven't any brothers and sisters either. There's only me. But then there's all the animals. Do you like animals?"

"I think I should very much," answered Anna, "but you can't have many animals in London."

"Well," said Daisy, who had now finished the last crumb of bread and the last drop of milk, "if you like, I'll show you my very own calf!"

"I'm afraid it's getting late," said Anna hesitatingly.

"'Twon't take you not five minutes altogether," said Daisy, scrambling hastily down from the gate. "Come along."

Anna followed her back to the farmyard, where she pushed open the door of a shed and beckoned her companion in. All was dim and shadowy, and there was a smell of new milk and hay. At first Anna could see nothing, but soon she made out, penned into a corner, a little brown calf with a white star on its forehead. It turned its dewy, dark eyes reproachfully upon them as they entered.

"You can stroke its nose," said its owner patronizingly.

"Shall you call it Daisy?" asked Anna, reaching over the hurdles to pat the soft, velvety muzzle.

"Mother says we mustn't have no more Daisies," said its mistress, shaking her little round head gravely. "You see, Puppa called all the cows Daisy, after me, for ever so long. There was Old Daisy and Young Daisy and Red Daisy and White Daisy and Big Daisy and Little Daisy and a whole lot more. So this one is to be called something different. Mother says Stars would be best."

As she spoke, a distant clock began to tell out the hour. Anna counted the strokes with anxiety. Actually seven! The dinner hour at Waverley, and whatever haste she made, she must be terribly late.

"Ah, I must go," she said. "I ought not to have stayed so long. Goodbye. Thank you."

"Come over again," said Daisy, calling after her as she ran to the gate. "Come at milking time, and I'll show you all the lot."

Anna nodded and smiled and ran off as fast as she could. This was her first transgression at the vicarage. What would Aunt Sarah say?

Chapter 6
Difficulties

No man can serve two masters.
MATTHEW 6:24

Anna found her life at Waverley bright and pleasant as the time went on, in spite of Aunt Sarah's strict rules and regulations. There was only one matter which did not become easy, and that was her nearer acquaintance with her grandfather. Somehow, when she asked to go to Dornton, there was always a difficulty of some kind—Mrs. Forrest could not spare the time to go with her, or the pony cart to take her, or a maid to walk so far, and she must not go alone. At first, mindful of her resolves, she made efforts to overcome those objections, but being always repulsed, she soon ceased them and found it easier and far more pleasant to leave her aunt to arrange the visits herself.

In this way they became very rare, and when they did take place, they were not very satisfactory, for Anna and her grandfather were seldom left alone. She did not, therefore, grow to be any fonder of Back Row or to associate her visits there with anything pleasant. Indeed, few as they were, she soon began to find them rather irksome and to be relieved when they were over. This was the only subject on which she was not perfectly

confidential to her new friend, Delia, who was now her constant
companion; for although Anna went very seldom to Dornton,
Mrs. Forrest made no objection to their meeting often else-
where.

So Delia would run over to the vicarage whenever she
could spare time or join Anna in long country rambles, and
on these occasions, it was she who listened and Anna who did
most of the talking. Delia heard all about her life in London
and how much better she liked the country, all about Aunt Sarah's punctuality and how difficult it was to go to Dornton, but
about the Professor she heard very little. Always on the lookout
for slights on his behalf, and jealous for his dignity, she soon
began to feel a little sore on his account and to have a suspicion
that Anna's heart was not in the matter. For her own part, she
knew that not all the aunts and rules in the world would have
kept her from paying him the attention that was his due. As the
visits became fewer, this feeling increased and sometimes gave
a severity to her manner which Anna found hard to bear, and
finally led to their first disagreement.

"Can you come over to church at Dornton with me this
evening?" asked Delia one afternoon as she and Anna met at
the stile halfway across the fields.

"I should like to," said Anna readily, "very much indeed, if
Aunt Sarah doesn't mind."

"I'll walk back with you as far as this afterwards," said
Delia. "You would see your grandfather. You've never heard
him play the organ yet."

"I don't *suppose* my aunt would mind," said Anna hesitatingly, her fair face flushing a little.

"Well," said Delia, "you can run back and ask her. I'll wait
for you here. You will just have time."

The bells of St. Mary's church began to sound as she spoke.

"Only you must go at once," she added, "or we shall be too
late."

Still Anna hesitated. She hated the idea of asking Aunt

Sarah and seeing her mouth stiffen into that hard line which was so disagreeable, but it was almost as bad to face Delia, standing there, bolt upright, with her dark eyes fixed so unflinchingly upon her.

"I know," she said appealingly, "that Aunt Sarah *has* arranged for me to go to Dornton next week."

"Oh," said Delia coldly.

"And," pursued Anna, turning away from her companion and stooping to pick a flower, "she does like me, you know, to go to the service at Waverley with her. She says Uncle prefers it."

Delia's glance rested for a moment in silence on the bending figure with the pale yellow hair outspread on the shoulders, gleaming in the sunshine. Then she said in a rather hard voice:

"The fact is, I suppose, you don't *want* to go. If so, you had better have said so at first."

Anna rose quickly and faced her friend.

"It's unkind, Delia," she exclaimed, "to say that. I *do* want to go. You know I like to be with you, and I should like to go to Dornton church much better than Waverley."

"Then why don't you ask Mrs. Forrest?" said Delia calmly. "She can't mind your going if I walk back with you. It's worth the trouble if you want to see your grandfather."

Anna cast down her eyes and fidgeted with the flowers in her belt.

"You don't understand," she began rather nervously, "how difficult it is to ask Aunt Sarah some things—"

"But this is quite a right, reasonable thing," interrupted Delia. "There's nothing wrong in wishing to see your grandfather sometimes. Of course, if you never ask Mrs. Forrest, she thinks you don't care about it."

"I do ask," said Anna. "I have often asked, but, you know I told you, Delia, Aunt Sarah never likes me to go to Dornton."

"Then you mean to give it up, I suppose," said Delia coldly.

"If I'm staying with Aunt Sarah, I suppose I ought to do

as she wishes," said Anna, "but, of course, I shan't give it up entirely. She doesn't wish me to do that."

Delia stood for a moment in silence, her eyes fixed on Anna's pretty, downcast face. The sound of the church bells came softly to them over the fields from Dornton. "Well," she said with a little sigh, "I mustn't stay or I shall be late, and I promised to meet the Professor after church. He half expects to see you with me. What shall I say to him?"

"Oh, Delia!" cried Anna, looking up into her companion's face, "I *do* wish I could go with you."

"It's too late now," said Delia, turning away. "Goodbye."

Anna lingered at the stile. Would not Delia turn around once and nod kindly to her as she always did when they parted? No. Her compact figure went steadily on its way, the shoulders very square, the head held high and defiantly. Anna could not bear it. She jumped over the stile and ran after her friend. "Delia!" she called out. Delia turned and waited. "Don't be cross with me," pleaded Anna. "After all, it isn't my fault, and I *should* like to go with you so much. And—and give my love to Grandfather, please. I'm going to see him next week."

She took hold of Delia's reluctant hand and kissed her cheek. Delia allowed the embrace but did not return it. Her heart was hot within her. Mrs. Winn had said that Anna was not straightforward. Was it true?

Anna had not much time for any sort of reflection, for she had to get back to Waverley as fast as she could; and, in spite of her haste, the bell stopped just as she reached the garden gate, and she knew that her aunt would have started for church without her. It was barely five minutes' walk, but she had to smooth her hair, and find some gloves, and make herself fit for Mrs. Forrest's critical eye, and all this took some time. When she pushed open the heavy door and entered timidly, her footfall sounding unnaturally loud, the usual sprinkling of evening worshippers was already collected, and her uncle had begun to read the service. Anna crept into a seat. She knew that she had committed a very grave fault in Mrs. Forrest's sight, and she half wished that she had made up her mind to go to Dornton with Delia. She wanted to please everyone, and she had pleased no one. It was hard. As she walked back to the vicarage with her aunt after service, she was quite prepared for the grave voice in which she began to speak.

"How was it you were late this evening, Anna?"

"I'm very sorry, Aunt," she answered. "I was talking to Delia Hunt in the field, and until we heard the bell, we didn't know how late it was."

"If you must be unpunctual at all," said Mrs. Forrest, "and I suppose young people will be thoughtless sometimes, I must beg that you will at least be careful not to let it occur at church time. Nothing displeases your uncle more than the irreverence of coming in late, as you did today. It is a bad example to the whole village, besides being very wrong in itself. As a whole," she continued after a pause, "I have very little fault to find with your behavior. You try to please me, I think, in every respect, but in this matter of punctuality, Anna, there is room for improvement. Now, you were a quarter of an hour late for dinner one night. You had been with Delia Hunt then too. I begin to think you run about too much with her. It seems to make you forgetful and careless."

"But," said Anna impulsively, "my being late had nothing at all to do with Delia that time. I was with Daisy Oswald."

"Daisy Oswald!" repeated Mrs. Forrest in a tone of surprise. "When did you make Daisy Oswald's acquaintance?"

She turned sharply to her niece with a searching glance. Anna blushed and hesitated a little.

"I—we—Delia and I met her father as we were walking home from Dornton. He asked me to go and see his cows, and then, after Delia had left me, I met his little girl in the lane just near the farm."

Mrs. Forrest was silent. She could not exactly say that there was anything wrong in all this, but she highly disapproved of it.

It was most undesirable that her niece should be running about the fields and lanes and picking up acquaintances in this way. Daisy Oswald was a very nice little girl, and there was no harm done at present, but it must not continue. The thing to do, she silently concluded, was to provide Anna with suitable occupations and companions which would make so much liberty impossible for the future.

To her relief, Anna heard no more of the matter, but it was easy to see that Aunt Sarah had not liked the idea of her being with Daisy. It was uncomfortable to remember that she had not been quite open about it. Somehow, since that first foolish concealment, she had constantly been forced into little crooked paths where she could not walk quite straight, but she consoled herself by the reflection that she had not told any untruth.

A few days later, Mrs. Forrest, returning from a drive with her face full of satisfaction, called Anna to her in her sitting room. She had been able, she said, to make a very nice arrangement for her to have some lessons in German and French with the Palmers. Miss Wilson, their governess, had been most kind about it, and it was settled that Anna should go to Pynes twice every week for a couple of hours.

"It will be an immense advantage to you," concluded Mrs. Forrest, "to learn with other girls, and I hope, besides the interest of the lessons, that you will make friendships which will be both useful and pleasant. Isabel Palmer is about your own age, and her sister is a little older. They will be nice companions for you, and I hope you will see a good deal of them."

From this time Anna's life was very much altered. Gradually, as her interests and amusements became connected with the Palmers and all that went on at their house, she saw less and less of Delia, and it was Mrs. Forrest who had to remind her when a visit to Dornton was due. There were no more country rambles, or meetings at the stile, and no more confidential chats. Anna had other matters to attend to, and if she were not occupied with lessons, there was always some engagement at Pynes which must be kept. And yet, she often thought, with a regretful sigh, there was really no one like Delia! Isabel Palmer was very pleasant, and there was a great deal she enjoyed very much at Pynes, but in her heart she remained true to her first friend. If only it had been possible to please everyone! If only Delia would be kind and agreeable when they did meet, instead of looking so cold and proud! By degrees Anna grew to dread seeing her, instead of looking forward to it as one of her greatest pleasures at Waverley. Everything connected with Pynes, on the contrary, was made so easy and pleasant. Aunt Sarah's lips never looked straight and thin when she asked to go there, and Isabel Palmer was sure of a welcome at any time. The pony cart could nearly always be had if it were wanted in that direction, though it seemed so inconvenient for it to take the road to Dornton. And then, with the Palmers there was no chance of severe looks on the subject of Mr. Goodwin. Did they know, Anna wondered, that he was her grandfather? Perhaps not, for they had lived at Pynes only a short time. There was no risk of meeting him there, for Saturday, when he gave Clara a music lesson, was an especially busy day with Mrs. Forrest, and she always wanted Anna at the vicarage.

It was strange that Anna should have come to calling it a "risk" to meet her grandfather, but it was true. Not all at once, but little by little, since her separation from Delia, the habit of dismissing him from her thoughts, as well as keeping silent about him, had grown strong within her. At first, Delia's scornful face often seemed to flash before her in the midst of some gaiety or enjoyment. "You are not worthy of him," it seemed to say. But it had been so often driven away that it now came very seldom, and when it did, it looked so pale and shadowy that it had no reality about it. Anna threw herself into the amusements which her new friends put in her way, and she determined to be happy in spite of uncomfortable recollections.

On her side, Delia had now come to the swift decision

natural to her age and character. Anna was unworthy. She had been tried and found wanting. Gold had been offered to her, and she had chosen tinsel. It was not surprising that the Palmers should be preferred to herself, but that anyone related to the Professor, able to see and know him, should be capable of turning aside and neglecting him for others was a thing she could neither understand nor bear with patience. She ceased to speak of it when she met Anna and preserved a haughty silence on the subject, but her manner and looks expressed disapproval plainly enough. The disapproval grew stronger as time went on, for although no word of complaint ever passed Mr. Goodwin's lips, Delia soon felt sure that he longed to see more of his grandchild. They often talked of Anna, the Professor listening eagerly to any news of her or account of her doings. No hint of disappointment was ever given, but affection has quick instincts, and Delia was able to understand her old friend's silence as well as his speech. She ran into No. 4 Back Row one afternoon and found him looking rather uncertainly and nervously at his tea table, which Mrs. Cooper had just prepared in her usual hurried manner—slapping down the cups and plates with a sort of spiteful emphasis and leaving the cloth awry. He looked relieved to see Delia.

"You would perhaps put things a little straight and make it look nicer," he said. "I don't know how it is, but Mrs. Cooper seems to spoil the look of things so."

"You expect a visitor?" said Delia as she began to alter the arrangement of the little meal and noticed two cups and plates.

"Yes," said the Professor, half shyly. "I got some water cresses and some free eggs. And that kind Mrs. Winn sent me some trout this morning. Mrs. Cooper promised to come in presently and cook them."

Delia observed that the room had quite a holiday air of neatness. There was no dust to be seen anywhere, and a special high-backed armchair, which was not in general use, was now drawn up to one side of the tea table.

"That was Prissy's chair," he continued, looking at it affectionately. "She always sat there, and I thought I should like to see Anna in it."

"Oh, is Anna coming to tea with you?" exclaimed Delia. "I *am* glad. Is she coming alone?"

The Professor nodded. There was a faint pink flush of excitement on his cheek. His hand trembled a little as he touched the bunch of mignonette which he had put on the table.

"My flowers never do very well," he said, trying to speak in an off-hand tone. "They don't get enough sun. And then, the other day I had to pour my coffee out of the window, and I forgot that the border was just underneath. I daresay it didn't agree with them."

"I suppose Mrs. Cooper made it so badly that even you could not drink it?" said Delia. "But it's certainly hard that she should poison your flowers as well. Why don't you tell her about it?"

"Oh, she does her best, she does her best," said the Professor quickly. "I wouldn't hurt her feelings for the world."

"Well, she won't improve at that rate," said Delia. "It's a good thing everyone is not so patient as you are. Now—" surveying her arrangements, "I think it all looks very nice, and as I go home, I'll call in at Mrs. Cooper's and remind her about the fish. Perhaps I shall have time to bring you a few more flowers before Anna comes."

Quite excited at the idea of the Professor's pleasure at having Anna all to himself for a little while, she quickly performed her errands and finally left him in a state of complete preparation, with roses upon his table and trout cooking in the kitchen. He himself, stationed at the window, meanwhile, pulled his watch out of his pocket every two or three minutes to see if it were time for his guest to arrive.

During the week which followed, Delia thought more kindly of Anna than she had done for some time past. Perhaps, after all, she had judged her too hastily; perhaps she had been hard and unjust. Very likely this meeting would be the beginning of a happier state of things between Mr. Goodwin and his grandchild.

"Did you have a pleasant evening on Saturday?" she asked when they next met.

Anna was sitting in the Palmers' pony cart, outside a shop in the town, waiting for Isabel. She blushed brightly when she saw Delia and looked rather puzzled at her question.

"Where?" she said vaguely. "Oh, I remember. I was to have had tea with my grandfather, but my aunt made another engagement for me, and I didn't go."

Delia's face clouded over with the disapproving expression Anna knew so well.

"He didn't mind a bit," she said, leaning forward and speaking earnestly. "He said another evening would do just as well for him."

"I daresay he did," replied Delia coldly.

"And, you see, it was a cricket match at Holmbury," Anna continued in an apologetic voice. "Such a lovely place! And the Palmers offered to drive me, and another day wouldn't have done for that, and Aunt Sarah thought—"

"Oh, naturally," said Delia lightly, "the cricket match was far more important. And, of course, the Professor wouldn't mind. Why should he?"

She nodded and passed on, just as Isabel came out of the shop.

"Wasn't that Delia Hunt?" said Isabel as she got into the pony cart. "What is the matter? Her face looked like the sky when thunder is coming."

Delia felt as she looked, as though a storm were rising within her. She thought of the Professor's little feast prepared so carefully, the flowers, and the high-backed chair standing ready for the guest who never came. She could not bear to imagine his disappointment. How could Anna be so blind, so insensible? All her hard feelings towards her returned, and they were the more intense because she could speak of them to no one—a storm without the relief of thunder. She had a half-dread of her next meeting with Mr. Goodwin, for with this resentment in her heart, it would be difficult to talk about Anna with patience, and yet the meeting must come very soon.

The next day was Wednesday, on which evening it was his custom to stay in the church after service and play the organ for some time. Delia, who was generally his only listener, would wait for him, and they would either stroll home together, or, if it were warm weather, sit for a little while under a certain tree near the church. They both looked forward to those meetings, but this week, when the time came, and Delia mounted the steep street which led up to the church, she almost wished that the Professor might not be there.

Dornton church was perched upon a little hill, so that, though it was in the town, it stood high above it, and its tall gray spire made a landmark for miles around. The churchyard, carefully planted with flowers and kept in good order, sloped sharply down to old gabled houses on one side, and on the other to open meadows, across which the tower of Waverley Church could be just seen amongst the trees. On this side a wooden bench, shadowed by a great ash, had been let into the low wall, and it was to this that Delia and the Professor were in the habit of retiring after the Wednesday evening services.

Mr. Goodwin's music had always power to soothe Delia and to raise her thoughts above her daily troubles, but tonight, as she sat listening to him in the empty church, she felt even more than usual as if a mighty and comforting voice were speaking to her. As long as the resounding notes of the organ continued, she forgot the little bustle of Dornton and her anger against Anna, and even when the Professor had finished and joined her on the porch, the calming influence remained.

"Can you stay a little this evening?" he asked as they walked through the churchyard together. "If you can spare

time, I should like a talk. It's about Anna," he continued when
they were seated under the flickering shadow of the ash tree. "I
didn't see her the other evening after all—"

"So I heard," said Delia.

"No—I didn't see her," repeated Mr. Goodwin, poking the
ground reflectively with his stick. "She went to some cricket
match with her friends. She's to come to me another time. It's
very kind of Mrs. Palmer to give her so much pleasure. I suppose Anna enjoys it very much? I hear of her going about with
them a good deal."

"I think she does," said Delia.

"It's always such a comfort to me," he continued, his kind
eyes beaming upon his companion from beneath the brim of
his wideawake, "to think that you are her friend. I don't see
much of her. I told you I should not be able to, when she first
came, but the next best thing is to know that you do."

Delia was silent. She did not meet his glance but pressed
her lips together and frowned a little.

"Anna wants a friend," pursued the Professor thoughtfully.
"Little as I see of her, I can tell that. She has the sort of nature
which depends greatly on influence—everyone does, I suppose, but some of us can stand alone better than others."

"Anna seems to get on very well," said Delia. "People always
like her."

"Yes, yes, yes," said the Professor, nodding his head gently,
"so I should think—so I should think. But when I say a 'friend,'
Delia, I don't mean that sort of thing. I mean someone who's
willing to take a little trouble."

"I don't see how you can be a friend to a person that doesn't
want you," said Delia impatiently. "If Anna wanted me—"

"You're not displeased with her about anything, I hope?"
said the Professor anxiously. "She has not offended you?"

Delia hesitated. She could not bear to disappoint him, as he
waited eagerly for her answer.

"The fact is," she said at length, "I don't understand Anna. She doesn't look at things in the same way as I do. She gets on better with the Palmers than with me."

"I'm sorry for that," said the Professor with a discouraged air, "but Anna's very young, you know, in years and character, too. I daresay she needs patience."

"I'm afraid I've not been patient," said Delia humbly.

Mr. Goodwin was the only person in the world to whom she was always ready to own herself in the wrong.

"Oh, well, patience comes with years," he said. "You're too young yet to know much about it. It's often hard enough, even after a long life, to bear with the failings of others, and to understand our own. People are so different. Some are strong, and some are weak. And the strong ones are always expecting the weak ones to stand upright, as they do, and go straight on their way without caring for praise or blame. And, of course, they can't. It's not in them. They stumble and turn aside at little things that the others wouldn't notice. And the weak ones, to whom, perhaps, it is natural to be sweet-tempered, and yielding, and forgiving, expect those virtues from the strong—and they don't find them—and then they wonder how it is that they find it hard to forgive and impossible to forget, and call them harsh and unbearable. And so we go on misunderstanding instead of helping each other."

Delia's face softened. Perhaps she had been too hasty with Anna—too quick to blame.

"Listen," said the Professor, "I was reading this while I waited for service to begin this evening."

He had taken out of his pocket a stumpy and very shabby little brown volume of Thomas à Kempis, which was very familiar to her.

"'But now, God hath thus ordered it, that we may learn to bear one another's burdens, for no man is without fault; no man but hath his burden; no man is self-sufficient; no man has wisdom enough for himself alone. But we ought to bear with one another, comfort, help, instruct, and admonish one another.'"

He shut the little book and turned his eyes absently across the broad, green meadows. Delia knew that absent look of the Professor's well. It meant that he was traveling back into the past, seeing and hearing things of which she knew nothing. Yet, though he did not seem to be speaking to her, every word he said sank into her mind.

"It's very hard for strong people to bear with weakness. It's such a disappointing, puzzling thing to them. They are always expecting impossibilities. Yet they are bound to help. It is a sin to turn aside—to leave weakness to trail along in the mire when they might be a prop for it to lean on and climb upwards by. The strong have a duty to the weak, lessons to learn from them. But they are hard lessons—hard lessons."

Long after he had finished, Mr. Goodwin sat with his eyes fixed musingly on the distance, and Delia would not disturb his thoughts by a single word. Even when they walked home together, they had very little to say and were both in a silent mood. When they parted at the turning to Back Row, Delia spoke almost for the first time.

"I'm not going to be cross to Anna anymore, Professor. You may feel quite happy about that."

Chapter 7
The Palmers' Picnic

Faithful are the wounds of a friend.
PROVERBS 27:6

One very hot afternoon a little later, there had been a glee practicing at the Hunts' house, a meeting which, of all others, was most distasteful to Delia. The last guest had taken leave, and her mother being on the edge of a comfortable nap in the shaded drawing room, she was just stealing away to her garret, when the bell rang.

"Don't go away, my love," murmured Mrs. Hunt, half-asleep, and as she spoke, Mrs. Winn's solid figure advanced into the room.

Delia resigned herself to listen to the disjointed chat which went on between the two ladies for a little while, but soon the visitor, taking pity on Mrs. Hunt's brave efforts to keep her eyes from closing, turned her attention in another direction.

"I'm afraid," she said, moving her chair nearer to Delia, "that poor old Mr. Goodwin must be sadly disappointed about his grandchild, isn't he?"

It always vexed Delia to hear the Professor called "poor" and "old."

"Why?" she asked shortly.

"Well, because he evidently sees so little of her," said Mrs. Winn. "It has turned out exactly as I said it would. I said from the very first, that sort of marriage never answers. It always creates discord. Of course, it's a difficult position for Mrs. Forrest, but she ought to remember that the child owes duties and respect to Mr. Goodwin. 'Honor thy father and mother,' and, of course, that applies to a grandfather, too."

"I believe Mr. Goodwin is quite satisfied," answered Delia.

"Oh, I daresay," said Mrs. Winn. "We all know he's a dear, meek, old man who could never say no to a goose. But that doesn't make it right. Now, I know for a fact that he expected Anna Forrest to tea with him one evening, and she never came. I know all about it because I happened to send him some trout that morning, and Mrs. Cooper went in to cook them. Mrs. Cooper chars for me, you know. 'I was quite sorry, ma'am,' she said when she came the next day, 'to see the poor old gentleman standing at the window with his watch in his hand, and the trout done to a turn, and his flowers and all. It's hard on the old to be disappointed.'"

Mrs. Winn rolled out these sentences steadily, keeping her eyes firmly fixed on Delia all the while. Now she waited for a reply.

"I heard about it," she said. "Anna was not able to go."

"Then she should have sent word sooner, or her aunt should have done so. It was a great want of respect. I'm surprised, Delia, you should take it so cooly when you think so much of Mr. Goodwin. Now, if *I* should see Anna Forrest, I shall make a point of putting her conduct in a right light to her. I daresay no one has done so yet—and she is but a child."

Delia shivered inwardly. She knew that Mrs. Winn was quite capable of doing as she said. How the Professor would shrink from such interference! Yet she did not feel equal to saying much against it, for Mrs. Winn had always kept her, and everyone else in Dornton, in order. Her right to rebuke and admonish was taken as a matter of course.

"You don't know, you see," she began, "how it was that Anna was prevented. Perhaps—"

Mrs. Winn had now risen and stood ready to depart, with her umbrella planted firmly on the ground.

"My dear," she interrupted, raising one hand, "I know *this*. Wrong is wrong, and right is right. That's enough for me, and always has been. Now, I won't disturb your dear mother to say goodbye, for I think she's dropped off. I'll go softly out."

She moved with ponderous care out of the room, followed by Delia, but she came to a stand again in the hall.

"You heard about this picnic of the Palmers?" she said inquiringly. "You're going, of course. It seems to be a large affair."

"I'm not quite sure," said Delia.

"Julia Gibbins came in this morning," continued Mrs. Winn, "quite excited about her invitation. She wanted to know what I meant to wear. Julia's so absurdly frivolous. She thinks as much of her dress as a girl of sixteen. 'At your age, my dear Julia,' I said to her, 'we need not trouble ourselves about that. You may depend on it; no one will notice what we have on. For myself, I shall put on my paisley shawl and my thickest boots. Picnics are always draughty and damp.' I don't think she quite liked it. Now, do you suppose the Palmers have asked Mr. Goodwin? Anna Forrest's so much there that I should *almost* think they would."

"Why not, as well as other people in Dornton?" asked Delia.

"He never goes to Waverley," said Mrs. Winn.

"That is by his own wish," said Delia quickly. "He has told me about that."

"Oh, indeed, by his own wish," repeated Mrs. Winn, her wide-open gray eyes resting thoughtfully upon Delia. "That's strange, with his grandchild staying there. However," with a parting nod as she moved slowly out, "we shall soon see about the picnic."

Delia smiled to herself as she watched her visitor's portly form disappear out of sight. How very little it would matter to the Professor whether the Palmers sent him an invitation or not! He would not even notice the absence of one. He had never cultivated the habit of feeling himself injured and was happily placed far above the miseries of fancied slights and neglect. Nevertheless she resented, as she always did, the tone of condescension with which Mrs. Winn had mentioned him, and she returned to the drawing room with a ruffled brow and a vexed spirit.

Mrs. Hunt still slumbered peacefully, quite undisturbed by the little agitations of Dornton. As her daughter entered, she gently opened her eyes.

"Del, my love," she murmured, "I meant to ask you to go and inquire how Mrs. Hurst's little boy is this morning. Did I?"

"No, Mother," said Delia.

"There's a beautiful jelly made for him," said Mrs. Hunt, closing her eyes again and folding her hands in front of her comfortable person. "I thought you might take it."

"I passed the door this morning," said Delia. "I could easily have taken it if you had remembered to ask me. It's so late now."

"It won't keep firm in this hot weather," continued Mrs. Hunt's sweet, low voice. "He ought to have it today."

Delia did not answer. She was tired. It was hot. Mrs. Winn's visit had come at the close of a most irksome afternoon. She was longing for a little quiet time for her music.

"Poor Mrs. Hurst!" pursued her mother. "So many children and so few to help her. Johnnie's been worse the last day or two."

As usual on such occasions, Delia shortly found herself, basket in hand, making her way along the dusty High Street to Mrs. Hurst's house. Dornton and the Dornton people seemed to her at that moment almost unbearable. Should she ever get away from them? she wondered. Would her life be spent within the hearing of Mrs. Winn's sententious remarks, the tedious discussions of tiny details, the eternal chatter and gossip, which still seemed to buzz in her ears from the meeting that afternoon? Then her thoughts turned to their usual refuge, the Professor, and she began to plan a visit to Anna at Waverley. Since her last talk with him, she had made up her mind that she would do her very utmost to renew their old friendliness. She would not take offense so easily, or be so quick to resent it, when Anna did not see things as she did. She would be patient, and she would keep her promise to the Professor. She would try to understand. For his sake she would humble herself to make the first advance, and this, for Delia's somewhat stubborn spirit, was a greater effort than might be supposed.

Anna, meanwhile, was quite as much interested as the Dornton people about the picnic which the Palmers intended to give. All country pleasures were new to her, and her companions at Pynes were very much amused to hear that she had never been to a picnic in her life and had most confused ideas as to what it meant.

"It will be a very large one," said Isabel Palmer to her one morning. "Mother thinks it will be such a good way of entertaining the Dornton people. We thought of a garden party, but if it's fine, a picnic will be much more fun."

The three girls were alone in the schoolroom, their lessons just over, and Anna was lingering for a chat before going back to Waverley.

"Have you settled on the place yet?" she asked.

"Alderbury," replied Isabel, "because it's near, and there's a jolly little wood to make the fire in."

"How delightful it will be!" exclaimed Anna. "How I wish it was going to be tomorrow. I'm so afraid something will prevent it."

"Bother this list!" put in Clara's voice from the table where she sat writing. "You might help me, Isabel."

"What do you want?" asked her sister.

"Well—Mr. Goodwin, for instance—am I to put him down?"

Anna gave a little start and gazed earnestly out of the window at which she stood, as Isabel went up to the table and looked over Clara's shoulder. Then they did not know! Aunt Sarah had not told them. How strange it seemed!

"W-well, I don't know," said Isabel reflectively. "We never have asked him to anything, but a picnic's different. He's a very nice old man, isn't he?"

"He's an old dear," replied her sister heartily, "but he's an organist. We shouldn't ask the organist of the church here."

"Mr. Goodwin's different somehow," said Isabel. "He's so clever, and then he's a great friend of the Hunts, you know, and, of course, we shall ask them."

"Well, what am I to do?" repeated Clara.

"Put him down, and put a query against him," decided Isabel, "and when mother sees the list, she can alter it if she likes."

Anna expected every moment during this discussion that her opinion would be asked. She stood quite still, her back turned to her companions, a bright flush on her cheek, her heart beating fast. When all chance of being appealed to was over, and the girls had gone on to other names, she drew a deep breath, as if she had escaped a danger.

"I must go now," she said, turning towards them. "Aunt Sarah wants me early today." And in a few moments, she was out of the house and on the way home.

It was not until she was halfway down the long hill which led from Pynes to Waverley that she began to realize what difficulties she had prepared for herself by her silence. If Mr. Goodwin were asked, and if he came to the picnic, the relationship between them must be known. That would not matter so much, but it would matter that she had seemed to be ashamed of it. Why had she not told them long ago? Why had she not spoken just now, at the first mention of his name? What a foolish, foolish girl she had been! What should she do now? Turning it over in her mind, she came to the conclusion that she must make some excuse to her Aunt and stay away from the picnic. She could not face what might happen there: the Palmers' surprise, Delia's scorn. "Why did you not tell us?" she heard them saying, and what could she answer? As she thought of how much she had looked forward to this pleasure, a few tears rolled down Anna's cheek, but they were not tears of repentance. She was only sorry for her own disappointment and because things did not go smoothly. It was very hard, she said to herself, and the hardest part was that she was forced continually into crooked ways. She did not want to be deceitful; she would much rather be brave and open like Delia, only things were too strong for her. As she thought this, Delia's face seemed suddenly to appear before her. It did not look angry or scornful, but had a gentle, almost pleasing expression on it. She was speaking, and what she said sounded quite clearly in Anna's ears. "Go back and tell them now. Go back and tell them now," over and over again.

Anna stopped uncertainly and turned her head to where, over the tops of the trees, she could still catch a glimpse of the chimneys of Pynes. She even took two or three steps up the hill again, the voice still sounding entreatingly and loud. But it was now joined by another, louder and bolder, which tried to drown it. This one told her that, after all, there was no need. Things would go well. The Palmers might never know. Soon they would go to Scotland, and after that—well, that was a long way off. Anna turned again, this time with decision, and finished the rest of her journey to Waverley almost at a run, without stopping to think anymore.

As the days went on without any further mention of Mr. Goodwin, she began to hope that, after all, she might be able to go to the picnic. How should she find out? She had not courage to ask the Palmers, and though it would have been a simple matter to ask her grandfather himself, she shrank from facing him and his gentle kindliness just now. If only some visitor from Dornton would come over! This wish was at last realized in a very unexpected way, and one which was not altogether pleasant. It was the day on which her visit to Mr. Goodwin was usually made, and she had begged her aunt to allow her to remain at home. The heat had given her a headache, and she would rather go to Dornton some other day. Mrs. Forrest received the excuse indulgently.

"I will call in and leave a message with Mr. Goodwin," she said, "and you had better lie down quietly in your own room. By the time I get back, you will be better, I hope."

But Aunt Sarah had hardly been gone ten minutes before there was a knock at Anna's door. It was the maidservant.

"Mrs. Winn would like to speak to you, miss. I told her you were not well, but she says she will only keep you a few minutes."

Anna did not know much of Mrs. Winn, and thought, as she went downstairs, that she had most likely some message for Mrs. Forrest to leave with her. Would she say anything about the picnic or the people who were going to it?

Mrs. Winn had taken up a determined position on a stiff, straight-backed chair in the middle of the room. There was severity in her glance as she replied to Anna's greeting and remarked that she was sorry to miss Mrs. Forrest.

"Aunt Sarah's only just started to drive into Dornton," said Anna. "I wonder you did not meet her."

"I came by the fields," replied Mrs. Winn shortly. "You were not well enough to go out, I hear?"

"I had a headache," said Anna, with her pretty blush. "Aunt thought I had better stay at home."

"You don't look much the worse for it," said Miss Winn without removing her unblinking gaze. "Girls in my young days didn't have headaches, or if they did, they put up with them and did their duty in spite of them. Things are turned topsy-turvy now, and it's the old who give way to the young."

Surprised at this tone of reproof, for which she was quite unprepared, Anna's usually ready speech deserted her. She said nothing, and she hoped that Mrs. Winn would soon go away. But that was evidently not her intention just yet. She had come prepared to say what was on her mind, and she would sit there until it was said.

"But perhaps," she continued, "it's just as well you didn't go out, for I've been wanting an opportunity to speak to you for some days."

"To me?" said Anna faintly.

"I never shrink from my duty," went on Mrs. Winn, "whether it's unpleasant or not, and I don't like to see other people doing so. Now, you're only a child, and when you neglect to do what's right, you ought to be told of it."

Anna gazed in open-eyed alarm at her visitor. What could be coming?

"I don't suppose you know, and, therefore, I think it my duty to tell you, that your grandfather, old Mr. Goodwin, was extremely disappointed the other day when you failed to keep your promise. I hear that he waited for you until quite late."

"Aunt Sarah wished me to go out with the Palmers," said Anna. "Grandfather said he didn't mind at all—"

"I knew your mother well," proceeded Mrs. Winn, rolling on her way without noticing this remark, "and a sweet young creature she was, though she made one mistake that I always regretted. And I know Mr. Goodwin, of course, and respect him, though he's not made of the stuff that gets on in the world. Still, whatever his position is, you owe him duty and reverence; and let me tell you, young lady, there may come a time when you'll be sorry you've not given it. It's all very well, and very natural, I daresay, to enjoy frolicking about with your fine young friends now. But youth passes, and pleasure passes, and then we all have time to remember the duties we didn't stoop to pick up when they lay at our door."

Anna sat in sulky silence during this long speech, with her eyes cast down and a pout on her lips. What right had Mrs. Winn to scold her?

Sullen looks, however, had no sort of effect on that lady, and when she had taken breath, she proceeded to finish her lecture.

"I keep my eyes open, and my ears, too, and I know very well that though your grandfather says nothing, and is the sort of man to bear any neglect without complaint, he feels hurt at your going so seldom to see him. And, knowing this, it was my duty to come and tell you, as there was no one else to do it. Your aunt and uncle are not intimate with him, and Delia Hunt's too young to speak with any weight. There's another thing, too, I wanted to mention. Up to yesterday, Mr. Goodwin had received no invitation to the Palmers' picnic."

Anna's heart gave a sudden leap of joy. Then she could go to the picnic!

"I fancy, if she knew this, that Mrs. Forrest would neither go herself nor allow you to do so," continued Mrs. Winn. "Considering his connection with this family, it's a slight to her and her husband as well as to him. It's extremely strange of the Palmers, when they take so much notice of you. I almost feel inclined to go on to Pynes this afternoon and point it out to them!"

She sat waiting, looking at Anna for a reply, but none came, for she was partly stunned by the force and suddenness of Mrs. Winn's attack and also filled with alarm at the idea of her going to Pynes. That would spoil everything. So, she sat in silence, nervously twitching her fingers in her lap, her downcast face strangely unlike that of the usually bright, self-possessed Anna.

"After all," concluded Mrs. Winn, "I'm rather tired, and it's a good mile farther, so I'll go back over the fields as I came, though the stiles do try me a good deal. You know how matters stand now, and you can't say you've not been openly dealt with. So we'll shake hands and bear no malice."

Anna went with her visitor as far as the garden door and watched her until she was hidden from sight by the great walnut tree on the lawn. What a tiresome, interfering old lady she was, and how angry Aunt Sarah would be! Her head really ached now. It felt as though someone had been battering it on each side with large, strong hands, and she was quite confused and giddy. But through it all, one triumphant thought came uppermost. She could go to the picnic! Presently she strolled out into the garden, fanning her hot face with her hat, as she turned things over in her mind. On the whole, she would not mention Mrs. Winn's visit to her aunt, and, of course, she must not know that Mr. Goodwin had not been asked to the picnic. It was very near now, and as Mrs. Forrest was not fond of listening to Dornton gossip, she was not likely to hear of it any other way. To go to the picnic had now taken such full possession of Anna's mind that nothing else seemed of much importance. She was ready to bend and twist everything that came in her way to make the road to it straight. A small reproving voice, which still sounded sometimes, was getting less and less troublesome. "Afterwards," Anna said to it, "after the picnic, I will behave differently. I will never conceal anything, and I will go often to see Grandfather—but I *must* go to the picnic."

The stable clock sounding five disturbed her reflections. Aunt Sarah would be home soon without fail, for at a quarter past there would be a mothers' meeting at the schoolroom, at which she always presided. Anna went too, sometimes, and helped to measure out calico and flannel, but she hoped she would be excused this afternoon. The schoolroom was hot, and she did not find the books Aunt Sarah read aloud to the mothers very interesting.

There was the pony cart in the distance! But who was the second figure sitting beside Mrs. Forrest? Could it be Delia? Anna ran through the house and onto the porch, from which she could see the long approach to the Rectory gate. There had been a time when Delia's coming had meant unmixed rejoicing, but that was over. She seemed to come now not so much as a friend but as a severe young judge, whose look condemned, even when she did not speak.

Mrs. Winn had only put into words what Delia's face had said for some time past, and, with the sound of them still in her ears, Anna felt more alarmed than pleased as she saw that it really was her old friend. Had she, too, come to point out her duty?

With the mothers' meeting on her mind, Mrs. Forrest descended quickly from the pony cart and passed Anna on the porch without looking at her.

"Is your headache better?" she said as she went straight into the drawing room, where tea was ready. "I overtook Delia on her way to see you and brought her on with me. You must take care of yourselves, for I must start almost immediately. Please pour me out a cup of tea at once."

When Mrs. Forrest had drunk her tea and set forth at a leisurely pace for the schoolroom, provided with work basket and book, the two girls were alone together. There was a pause of embarrassment, which Delia was the first to break.

"I was coming over," she said, "to ask if you would care to go and get water lilies down at the river this evening. You said you would like some rushes too."

Her voice sounded kind, almost as it used to long ago, although there was a sort of shyness in her manner. Anna was greatly relieved. Surely Delia would not have begun like this if she intended to reprove her.

"Mrs. Forrest said you might go, if your head was better," continued Delia.

Anna replied eagerly that her headache was nearly gone, a walk would do it good, and she should like it immensely; and a few minutes later, the girls started on their expedition. It was one which had been planned in the first days of their acquaintance, when Anna had thought no pleasure could compare to a ramble in the country with Delia. Fresh from the rattle and noise of London, its stony pavements, and the stiff brilliancy of the flowers in the parks, it had been a sort of rapture to her to wander freely over the fields and through the woods. Aunt Sarah's garden was beautiful, but this was better still. All the flowers found here might be gathered, and Delia knew exactly where they all grew in their different seasons and the best way of getting to them. Anna had begun, under her guidance, to make a collection of wild flowers, but, though started with great energy, it had not gone far. It had ceased, together with the walks, shortly after her acquaintance with the Palmers had filled her mind with other things. Yet those rambles with Delia had never been forgotten. Anna thought of them often and knew in her heart that she had never been so really happy since. This evening, as she walked along swinging her basket, she felt as though the old days had come back, and the old Delia too. It could not be so, really. If she knew—but she did not know. Meanwhile, the sky was blue, Delia was kind, the meadows were gay and pleasant, and she would forget everything disagreeable and enjoy herself.

Their way lay for a short distance along the high road, then over a stile, and down through the rich flat water meadows which spread out on each side of the river. The Dorn was neither a rapid nor a majestic stream, but it took its leisurely course between its sloping banks, with a contented ripple, disturbing no one. This course was a very winding one, making all kinds of little creeks and shallows and islands on its way, and these were full of delightful plants for anyone who cared to gather them. Tall families of bulrushes and reeds swayed to the wind whistling through them. Water lilies held up their flat green hands to make a table for their white blossoms. Forests of willow-herb on the banks, wild peppermint and comfrey, and the blue eyes of forget-me-nots peeped out here and there with modest confidence.

"There's an old punt fastened just about here," said Delia as they reached the river, "so we can get right out amongst the lilies, and then we can reach the rushes too."

Delia was always the leader on such occasions, and Anna was used to following her with perfect confidence, but when they came to the old punt, a little higher up, she eyed it with some misgivings. It looked very insecure, and shaky, and rotten.

"Oh, Delia," she cried as her companion jumped lightly onto it and waited for her to follow, "it's leaking—I can see the water through it. Do you think it will bear us both?"

Delia laughed as Anna crept cautiously down the bank. It reminded her of the time when she had had to encourage and help her to climb gates and scramble through hedges.

"Come along," she said, holding out her hand, "it's as safe as dry land. Why, I've seen four great boys on it at once."

"How beautiful!" cried Anna as, after a little more encouragement, she found herself safely on the punt by Delia's side, surrounded by water lilies and bulrushes. They set to work to fill their basket with these, and when it was done there were always finer ones still almost out of reach. These must be had at any cost. Delia would lie flat on the punt, while Anna held the skirt of her dress, and would manage to get hold of them with the handle of a stick. There was both excitement and triumph in these captures, and while they were going on, the girls forgot that any coolness had come between them, or that the world held much beyond water lilies and bulrushes. When, however, they climbed out of the punt with their dripping prizes and sat down on the bank to rest a little, recollections returned.

"What a pity," thought Anna with a sigh, "that things are not always pleasant. Delia is nicer than anyone when she is kind."

Delia, on her side as she packed the lilies into the basket, reminded herself that there was something she had to say to Anna, and she wondered how she should begin.

As usual, she plunged straight into the matter of which her mind was full, and said suddenly:

"Do you ever meet your grandfather at Pynes?"

Here was the tiresome subject again! All pleasure was over now.

"No, never," replied Anna. "He gives Clara lessons on Saturdays, and Aunt Sarah always wants me at home then."

"You are going to this picnic, I suppose?" said Delia. "Does Mrs. Forrest know that the Professor has not been asked?"

"I don't know," murmured Anna.

She glanced quickly at her companion and saw the severe look coming back which she always dreaded.

"Of course," continued Delia, "it does not in the least matter, as far as he is concerned, for he would not, in any case, go; but I should have thought his relations would have felt it a slight, and I can't understand Mrs. Palmer."

Anna was silent. She wished now that Delia had not come, though she had enjoyed the walk so much.

"But I didn't mean to talk about that," resumed Delia with an effort. "What I wanted to say had nothing to do with the picnic. It's about you, Anna, and myself."

"About me?" repeated Anna.

After all, Delia *was* going to be angry, yet her voice sounded quite soft and kind.

"Yes. At first I didn't mean to say anything to you because I thought you ought to be able to see it for yourself. And when you didn't, I was angry, and that kept me silent. But I know now, it was wrong. People can't see things just alike, and I ought to have been kinder and tried to help you more."

At this new tone of humility, Anna's heart softened at once to her friend. When she spoke like that, she felt for the moment that she would do anything she asked—even give up the picnic.

"Oh, Delia," she exclaimed impulsively, "you've always been very kind. Kinder than I deserve."

"That's nothing to do with it," answered Delia. "People can do without friends when they deserve them. The thing is, that I promised the Professor to be your friend, and I haven't carried it out."

"It's been my fault," said Anna in a penitent voice, "but really and truly, Delia, you may not believe me, but I *do* like you better than Isabel Palmer—or anyone. I do indeed."

She spoke the truth. At that moment she felt that she would rather have Delia for a friend than anyone in the world. Yet she was conscious that, if Delia knew all, she would find it hard to forgive her. What a pity it all was!

"So, what I want to tell you," continued Delia, "and what I ought to have told you before, is this. I've let you think that your grandfather doesn't mind your going so seldom to see him—but I know that he does."

She paused and looked earnestly at Anna.

"Grandfather never says anything about it," Anna murmured.

"That's just it," said Delia. "He's so unselfish and good, he wouldn't let you or anyone know it for the world. He thinks so little of himself, it would be impossible to offend him. It's not what he *says*. Oh, Anna, if you really knew, and loved him, you *couldn't* let anything else come before him! Not all the Palmers, and Waverleys, and Aunt Sarahs in the world. You *couldn't* give him a minute's pain or disappointment."

She was so moved by her subject that the tears stood in her dark eyes as she turned them upon Anna.

"I'll try, Delia. I really will," said the latter, "but it *is* hard. Harder than you think. It makes Aunt Sarah different for days afterward."

Delia snapped off the head of a water lily in her impatient fingers.

"Aunt Sarah!" she repeated. Then more gently, "You see, Anna, you must choose whether you'll pain the Professor or displease Mrs. Forrest. You can't possibly please both of them. You must choose which you think is right and stick to it. You can't serve God and mammon."

How dreadfully earnest Delia was! It almost frightened Anna to hear her talk like that.

"I will try," she repeated. "I will do my best, Delia, if only you won't be angry any longer."

She put her hand softly into her companion's, and Delia's fingers closed over it in a warm clasp. For the time, the old feelings of confidence and affection had returned, and when, a little later, Anna walked back to the vicarage alone, she was full of good resolves. She would try to deserve Delia's friendship. She would go often to Dornton and be very loving to her grandfather. She would turn over a new leaf.

"My dear Anna," cried Mrs. Forrest, meeting her on the porch with her basket of wet, shining river plants, "do you know the time? Miss Stiles has been waiting to try on your dress for the picnic. Dear me! What dripping things! Let Mary take them."

The picnic! Anna had really for the moment forgotten the picnic. All the good resolve trooped into the background again while she tried on the new dress. But only till *after* the picnic! When that was over, she would make a fresh start and never, never, conceal anything again.

Chapter 8
The Best Things

A rose which falleth from the hand, which fadeth in the breast,
Until in grieving for the worst, we learn what is the best.

MRS. BROWNING

Everything went on quite smoothly until the day fixed for the picnic came. Aunt Sarah gave no hint of any objection; the weather was gloriously hot and fine; Anna's new white dress was very pretty—there was nothing wanting to her long-desired enjoyment.

She stood amongst the nodding roses on the porch, waiting for the Palmers to call for her in their carriage, on the way to Alderbury. Aunt Sarah was, perhaps, to drive over and join the party later. Anna had dismissed all troublesome thoughts. She felt sure she was going to be very happy and that nothing unlucky would happen to spoil her pleasure. She was in gay spirits as she fastened a bunch of the little cluster roses in her dress. Isabel had once told her that she looked very pretty in white, and she was glad to feel that she suited the beauty of the bright summer day.

"Anna!" said Mrs. Forrest's voice from the hall within.

Anna turned. The hall looked dark and shadowy after the sunshine, but it was easy to see that there was vexation on her aunt's face as she studied the letter in her hand.

"I have just had a note from Dr. Hunt," she said. "Mr. Goodwin, your grandfather, is not very well."

"What is the matter?" asked Anna.

She left the porch and went up to her aunt's side.

"Why, I can't quite make it out. Dr. Hunt talks of fever, but he says there is nothing infectious. Brought on by overexertion in the heat, he thinks. He says you may safely go to see him—"

There was a pause. Mrs. Forrest and Anna looked at each other. Each waited for the other to speak. *Must I give up the picnic after all?* thought Anna.

"I don't gather that it's anything serious," said Mrs. Forrest at length. "I think the best plan will be for me to go over to Dornton, after you've started, and see Dr. Hunt. Then, if there's really no danger of infection, you can go there early tomorrow."

She looked inquiringly at Anna, as though half-expecting her to make some other suggestion. The sound of wheels on the gravel, and the tramp of horses, told that the Palmers were approaching. The wagonette, full of happy young people, drove up to the porch.

"Are you ready, Anna?" called out Isabel's voice.

"Will that satisfy you?" said Mrs. Forrest. "You must decide now."

"We're late, Anna," said Isabel again. "Why don't you come?"

Anna hesitated. She looked out at the bright sunshine, where her companions called her to gaiety and pleasure, and then at the letter in her aunt's hand.

"Here's your cloak, Miss Anna," said the maid waiting at the door.

In another moment, it seemed almost without any will of her own, she was squeezed into the carriage amongst her laughing companions, had waved a farewell to Mrs. Forrest standing smiling on the porch, and was whirled away to the picnic.

The hours of the sunny day, filled with delight for Anna

amongst the pleasant woods of Alderbury, did not pass so
quickly at No. 4 Back Row. The Professor was ill. He had had
a slight feverish attack to begin with, which passed off and
seemed of no importance, but it had left him in a state of
nervous weakness and prostration, at which Dr. Hunt looked
grave. Mr. Goodwin must have been overexerting himself
for some time past, he declared, and this breakdown was the
result. It would probably be some time before he could do any
work. Perfect rest, and freedom from all care and agitation,
were the only remedies.

"Don't let him know, Delia," he said to his daughter as he left
the house, "that he's likely to be laid up long. Keep him as quiet
and cheerful as possible. I'll send a line to Mrs. Forrest and let
her know that his grandchild may be with him as much as she
likes."

Delia prepared to spend the rest of the day with her old
friend, and having persuaded him to lie down on the hard little
couch, and having made him as comfortable as she could with
pillows, she sat down in the window with her sewing. From
here she could watch the little gate and prevent anyone from
entering too suddenly. Of course, Anna would come soon. The
Professor was very quiet, but she thought he turned his eyes
towards the door now and then, as though looking for someone. Was it Anna? At last, she was thankful to see him fall into
a doze which lasted some while, and she was just thinking for
the hundredth time that Anna *must* come now, when she was
startled by his voice.

"Prissy," it said quite clearly.

Delia went up to the sofa. Mr. Goodwin gazed at her for a
moment without recognition.

"You've had a nice sleep, Professor," she said smiling, "and
now you are going to have some tea with me."

But in spite of his sleep, the Professor's face looked anxious,
and he hardly tasted the tea which Delia prepared. As she took
his cup, he said wistfully:

"Did Dr. Hunt write to Mrs. Forrest?"

Delia nodded.

"Did—did Anna happen to come while I was asleep?" was his next question.

"She's not been here yet," said Delia, "but they may not have had the letter till late. She will come soon."

"I should like to see her," said the Professor.

Why did not Anna come? As the weary hours went by, and the sun got lower and lower, he became very restless. He looked first at his watch and then at the door and no longer tried to conceal how much he wanted to see his grandchild. Delia tried in vain to divert his mind by reading his favorite books, but it was evident that he was not listening to her. He was listening for the click of the gate and the footsteps outside. Every subject in which she tried to interest him came back to the same thing—Anna and Anna's doings. Delia could not help one throb of jealous pain as she recognized how powerless she was to take her place, a place she seemed to value so little. But it was only for a moment; the next she put all thought of herself aside. Anna belonged to the dearest of memories of the Professor's life. She had a place in his heart which would always be kept for her, whatever she had done or left undone. To bring peace and comfort to his face again, Delia would have been willing at that moment to give up her own place in his affections entirely. If only Anna would come!

"I suppose it's too late to expect her now, my dear, isn't it?" said the patient voice again.

Delia could not bear it any longer.

"I think," she said, as cheerfully as she could, "if you don't mind being alone a little while, I'll just run over to Waverley. Mrs. Cooper's here, if you want anything, you know."

"Will you really?" said the Professor, with hope in his voice.

"There's perhaps been some mistake about that letter," said Delia. "You'd like to see Anna tonight, wouldn't you?"

"Well, I *should*," said Mr. Goodwin. "It's very absurd, I know, but I had such a strange dream just now about her and Prissy,

and I can't get it out of my head. I suppose being not quite up
to the mark makes one unreasonable, but I really don't think I
could sleep without seeing her. It's very good of you to go, my
dear."

"I'll be back in no time, and I'll bring her with me," said
Delia.

She spoke with confidence, but halfway across the fields
she stopped her rapid pace, checked by a sudden thought—the
picnic!

In her anxiety she had forgotten about it. Anna might
have started before Dr. Hunt's note got to Waverley. Even then,
though, she said to herself, she must be home by now. So she ran
on again, and half an hour later she was on her way back over
the darkening fields—without Anna. She had gone to the picnic,
and she knew the Professor was ill! Once Delia would have felt
angry. Now, there was only room in her heart for one thought,
"He will be disappointed, and he will not sleep tonight."

The church clock struck nine as she entered the High Street
in Dornton, and the same sound fell faintly on Anna's ears
on her way back from Alderbury. The picnic had been over
long ago, but shortly after the party started to return, one of
the horses lost a shoe. The carriage in which Anna was had to
proceed at a slow walk for the rest of the distance, and it would
be very late before she could reach Waverley.

No accident, however, could dampen her spirits, or those of
her companions. It was all turned into amusement and fun. The
whole day had been more delightful than any Anna had known.
It was over now, that delightful day, and she gave a little sigh
of regret to think that she was at the end of it instead of at the
beginning. The one shadow which had fallen across the bright-
ness of it had been cast by the substantial figure of Mrs. Winn,
whom she had seen in the distance now and then. Once she had
noticed her in earnest conversation with Mrs. Palmer, and she
thought that they both looked in her direction, but it had been
easy to avoid contact with her amongst so many people. It had

not spoiled her enjoyment then, but now, her excitement a little cooled down, unpleasant thoughts began to make themselves heard.

Here was the Rectory at last! Anna burst into the drawing room, her fair hair falling in confusion over her shoulders, a large bundle of foxgloves in her arms, her cheeks bright with the cool night breeze.

"Oh, Aunt!" she exclaimed, "We've had such a lovely, lovely day. Why didn't you come?"

"You're very late, my dear Anna," said Mrs. Forrest gravely. "I expected you more than an hour ago."

Anna explained the reason of her delay.

"Alderbury is the most perfect place," she repeated. "Why didn't you come?"

"It's very unlucky that you should be so late," said Mrs. Forrest. "Delia has been over asking for you."

Anna's face fell. "Oh!" she exclaimed. "My grandfather! Is he worse?"

"I don't think so. And from what I learned from Dr. Hunt, he is not at all seriously ill. But he was restless, Delia said, and wanted to see you tonight."

"To see *me*!" said Anna. She let her flowers fall in a heap on the ground. "Oh, Aunt Sarah, I wish I had not gone to the picnic!"

"Now, my dear Anna, that is foolish. You shall go to Dornton early tomorrow, and no doubt you will find Mr. Goodwin better. Remember, there is no cause for anxiety, and though the accident of your being late was very unfortunate, it could not be avoided."

Aunt Sarah's composed words were reassuring. Probably her grandfather was not very ill, Anna thought, but oh, why had she gone to the picnic, and what would Delia say?

These last words were in her mind again next morning as she arrived at No. 4 Back Row and stood waiting to be let in. The little house looked very sad and silent, as though it knew its master was ill. Presently the door opened a very little way, and the long, mournful face of Mrs. Cooper appeared. When she saw who it was, she put her finger on her lip and then said in a loud, hoarse whisper, "I'll call Miss Delia."

Anna was left outside. She felt frightened. Why did Mrs. Cooper look so grave? Perhaps Grandfather was very ill after all!

It seemed ages before the door opened again, and when it did, it was Delia who stood there. She did not look at all angry, but her face was very sad.

"He has had a very bad night," she whispered, "but now he is sleeping. He must not be disturbed. You had better come later."

That was all. The door was gently shut again, and Anna stood outside. As she turned away, her eyes filled with tears. Yesterday her grandfather had wanted her, and she had not gone. Today the door was shut. He must be very ill, she felt sure, whatever Aunt Sarah might say. His kind, gentle face came before her as she made her way along—always kind, never with any reproach in it. How could she have gone to the picnic and left him to ask for her in vain?

As she reached the place where the pony cart waited for her, Isabel Palmer came out of a shop. She looked at her with a sort of cold surprise.

"Oh, Anna," she said, "how is Mr. Goodwin? We only heard yesterday he was ill. I was going to his house to ask after him."

"Dr. Hunt says there is no cause for anxiety," said Anna, repeating the sentence she had so often heard from Aunt Sarah.

"It was Mrs. Winn who told mother he was ill," continued Isabel, observing Anna's downcast face curiously. "And—she said another thing which surprised us all very much. Why didn't you tell us long ago that Mr. Goodwin is your grandfather?"

Anna was silent.

"We can't understand it at all," continued Isabel. "Mother says it might have caused great unpleasantness. She's quite vexed."

She waited a moment with her eyes fixed on Anna, and then said, with a little toss of her head, "Well—goodbye. I suppose we shan't meet again before we go to Scotland. Mother has written to tell Mrs. Forrest that we're not going on with lessons."

They parted with a careless shake of the hands, and Anna was driven away in the pony cart. Her friendship with Isabel and her pleasant visits to Pynes were over now. She was humbled and disgraced before everyone, and Delia would know it, too. It would have been a wounding thought once, but now there was no room in her heart for any feeling but dread of what might happen to Mr. Goodwin.

"Oh, Aunt Sarah," she cried when she reached Waverley and found her aunt in the garden, "I'm sure my grandfather is worse—I'm sure he's very ill. I did not see him."

Mrs. Forrest was tying up a rebellious creeper, which wished to climb in its own way instead of hers. She finished binding down one of the unruly tendrils before she turned to look at her niece. Anna was flushed. Her eyelids were red and swollen.

"Why didn't you see him?" she asked. "Does Dr. Hunt think him worse?"

"I don't know," said Anna. "I only saw Delia for a minute. He was asleep. I am to go again. Oh, Aunt Sarah," with a burst of sobs, "I do wish I had not gone to the picnic. I wish I had behaved better to my grandfather. I wish—"

Mrs. Forrest laid her hand kindly on Anna's shoulder.

"My dear," she said, "you distress yourself without reason. We can rely on Dr. Hunt's opinion that your grandfather only needs rest. Sleep is the very best thing for him. When you go this evening, you will see how foolish you have been. Meanwhile, try to exercise some self-control; occupy yourself, and the time will soon pass."

She turned to her gardening again, and Anna wandered off alone. Aunt Sarah's calm words had no comfort in them. Delia's severest rebuke, even Mrs. Winn's plain speech, would have been better. She went restlessly up to her bedroom, seeking she hardly knew what. Her eyes fell on the little brown case, long unopened, which held her mother's portrait. Words, long unthought of, came back to her as she looked at it.

"If you are half as good and beautiful," her father had said. And on the same day, what had been Miss Milverton's last warning? "Try to value the best things."

"Oh," cried Anna to herself as she looked at the pure, truthful eyes of the picture, "if I only could begin again! But now it's all got so wrong, it can never, never be put right!"

After a while, she went into the garden again; and avoiding Mrs. Forrest, she crossed the little footbridge leading into the field and sat down on the gate. The chimneys of Leas Farm in the distance made her think of Daisy and the old days when they had first met. She had been so full of good resolves. Daisy, and the good resolves, and Delia too, seemed all to have vanished together. She had no friends now. Everyone had deserted her, and she had deserved it!

She was sitting during those reflections, with her face buried in her hands, and presently was startled by the sound of a little voice behind her.

"What's the matter?" it said.

It was Daisy Oswald who had come through the garden and now stood on the bridge close to her, a basket of eggs in her hand, and her childish, freckled face full of wonder and sympathy.

Generally, Anna would have been ashamed to be seen in distress and would have tried to hide it, but now she was too miserable to mind anything. She hid her face in her hands again, without answering Daisy's question.

"Has someone been cross?" inquired Daisy at last.

Anna shook her head. Her heart ached for sympathy even from Daisy, though she could not speak to her, and she hoped she would not go away just yet.

"Have you hurt yourself?" proceeded Daisy.

Again, the same sign.

"Have you done something naughty? I did something naughty once."

Seeing that Anna did not shake her head this time, she added, in her condescending little tone, "If you like, I'll come sit beside you and tell you all about it."

She put her basket of eggs very carefully on the ground and placed herself comfortably by Anna's side.

"It was a very naughty thing *I* did," she began in a voice of some enjoyment, "worse than yours, I expect. It was a year ago, and one of our geese was sitting, and mother said she wasn't to be meddled with nohow. And the white Cochin-China hen was sitting too, and—" Daisy paused to give full weight to the importance of the crime and opened her eyes very wide, "and—I changed 'em! I carried the goose and put her on the hen's nest, and she forsook it, and the hen forsook hers, and the eggs were all addled! Mother *was* angry! She said it wasn't the eggs she minded so much as the disobedience. Was yours worse than that?"

"Much, much worse," murmured Anna.

Daisy made a click with her tongue to express how shocked she felt at this idea.

"Have you said you're sorry and you won't do it anymore?" she asked. "When you're sorry, people are kind."

"I don't deserve that they should be kind," said Anna, looking up mournfully at her little adviser.

"Father and mother were kind afterward," said Daisy. "I had to be punished though. I didn't have eggs for breakfast for a whole month after I changed the goose. I like eggs for breakfast," she added thoughtfully. Then, glancing at her basket as she got down from the gate, "Mother sent those to Mrs. Forrest. I came through the garden to find you, but I'm going back over the field. You haven't been to see Star for ever so long. She's becoming a real beauty."

Long after Daisy was out of sight, her simple words lingered in Anna's mind. They had made her feel less miserable, though nothing was altered. "When you're sorry, people are kind," she repeated. If her grandfather knew the very worst, if he knew that she had actually been ashamed of him, would he possibly forgive her? Would he ever look kindly at her again? Anna sat up and dried her tears. She lifted her head with a sudden resolve. "I will tell him," she said to herself, "every bit about it, from the very beginning, and then I must bear whatever he says and whatever Delia says."

It was easy to make this brave resolve with no one to hear it but the quiet cows feeding in the field, but when the evening came and she stood for the second time at No. 4 Back Row, her heart beat quickly with fear. When she thought of her grandfather's kind face, her courage rose a little, but when she thought of what she had to tell him, it fell so low that she was almost inclined to run away. The door opened, but this time Mrs. Cooper did not leave her outside. She flung open the door of the sitting room with her other hand and said in a loud voice, "Miss Forrest, sir."

Anna entered, half afraid as to what she should see, for she had made up her mind that her grandfather was really very ill. To her relief, the Professor and his shabby little room looked unaltered. He was sitting in his armchair by the window, tired and worn, as she had often found him before after one of his long walks, and he held out his kind hand to welcome her as usual.

"Oh, my dear Anna," he said, "you've come to see me. That's right. Come and sit here."

There was a chair close to him, and as she took it, Anna noticed a piece of half-finished knitting on the table, which she knew belonged to Delia. "If Delia comes in," she thought to herself, "I *can't* do it."

"Are you better, Grandfather?" she managed to ask, in a very subdued voice.

"Oh, I'm getting on splendidly!" he answered. "With such a good nurse, and so much care and attention, I shall soon be better than ever I was before."

There was no mistaking the expression in his face as he turned it towards her. Not only welcome and kindness, but love, shone from it brightly. In the midst of her confusion, Anna wondered how it was that she had never felt so sure of her grandfather's affection before. And now, perhaps, she was to lose it.

"You can't think how wonderfully kind everyone is," he continued. "I really might almost think myself an important person in Dornton. They send messages and presents and are ready to do anything to help me. Mr. Hurst came in just now to tell me that he has arranged to fill my place as organist for a whole month so that I may have a rest. They're very nice, good people in Dornton. That kind Mrs. Winn offered to come and read to me, and then Delia is like another granddaughter, you know."

Anna's heart was full as he chatted on. Must she tell him? Might she not put it off a little?

"And so you went to a picnic yesterday?" he went on as she sat silently by him. "Was it very pleasant? Let me see, did the sun shine? You must tell me all about it. I am to be an idle man now, you know, and shall want everyone to amuse me with gossip."

"Grandfather," cried Anna, with a sudden burst of courage, "I want to tell you—I've done something very wrong."

The Professor turned his gentle glance on her.

"We all have to say that, my dear," he answered, "very often. But I'm sure you're sorry for it, whatever it is."

"It's something very bad," murmured Anna. "Delia knows. She won't forgive me, I know, but I thought perhaps you would."

"Is it to Delia you have done wrong?" asked Mr. Goodwin.

"No. To you," replied Anna, gaining courage as she went on. "I—"

The Professor stroked her fair hair gently. It was just the same color as Prissy's, he thought.

"Then I don't want to hear any more, my dear," he said, "for I know all about it already."

The relief was so great, after the effort of speaking, that Anna burst into tears, but they were tears full of comfort and had no bitterness in them.

"Oh, Grandfather," she sobbed, "you *are* good. Better than anyone. I will never, never—"

"Hush, my dear, hush," said the Professor, patting her hand gently and trying to console her by all the means in his power.

"I wonder where Delia is!" he said at last, finding that his efforts were useless.

Anna sat up straight in her chair at the name and dried her tears. She dreaded seeing Delia, but it must be faced.

"She was here the moment before you came in," he continued. "Call her, my dear."

It was not possible to be very far off in Mr. Goodwin's house, and Delia's voice answered from the kitchen when Anna opened the door and called her. A few minutes afterward, she came into the room carrying a tray full of tea things. Her quick glance rested first on Anna's tearstained face and then on the Professor.

"Anna and I have had a nice talk, my dear Delia," he said with an appealing look, "and now we should all like some tea."

Delia understood the look. She put down her tray, went promptly up to Anna, and kissed her.

"Come and help me to get the tea ready," she said. "It's quite time the Professor had something to eat."

So Anna was forgiven, and it was in this way that, during her visit to Waverley, she began dimly to see what the best things are, and to see it through sorrow and failure. It was a lesson she had to go on learning, like the rest of us, all through her life—not an easy lesson, or one to be quickly known. Sometimes we put it from us impatiently and choose something which looks more enticing and not so dull, and for a time we go on our way gaily—and then, a sorrow, or perhaps a sin, brings home to us that everything is worthless compared to Love, Truth, and Faithfulness to Duty, and that if we have been false to them, there is no comfort anywhere until we return to serve them with tears of repentance.

The End

More Books from The Good and the Beautiful Library!

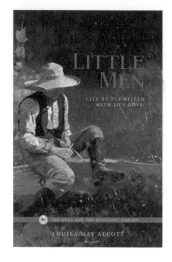

Little Men
by Louisa May Alcott

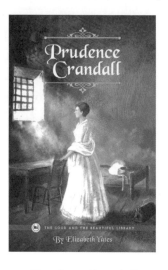

Prudence Crandall
by Elizabeth Yates

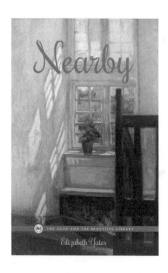

Nearby
by Elizabeth Yates

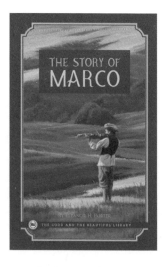

The Story of Marco
by Eleanor H. Porter

www.thegoodandthebeautiful.com